"What about you, Agent Buchanan? How did you become a rescue and retrieval specialist?"

"I have a knack for putting people at ease and making them believe what I want them to believe. I make the bad guy believe he's going to get one thing and then I do exactly the opposite of what he expects."

He chuckled—couldn't help himself. This was a woman who enjoyed her work.

"Well, Agent Buchanan, it's a pleasure to make your acquaintance." He thrust his hand at her.

She grinned and gave it a shake. "Ditto, Agent Flynn."

Now if they could only get themselves out of this thorny situation, maybe he'd ask her out to dinner.

A frown furrowed his brow. The beef jerky obviously hadn't done its job or he wouldn't still be thinking about food.

Then again, maybe it wasn't food on his mind.

He peeked at the lady lying so close.

Too dangerous, he reminded himself.

Maybe another time when they weren't both targeted for execution.

THE SAFEST LIES

USA TODAY Bestselling Author

DEBRA WEBB

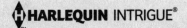

HARLEQUIN INTRIGUE®

This book is dedicated to my two beautiful daughters. Like the
heroine in this book, you are strong, amazing women!

ISBN-13: 978-1-335-60459-0

The Safest Lies

Copyright © 2019 by Debra Webb

Recycling programs
for this product may
not exist in your area.

Printed in U.S.A.

™ www.Harlequin.com

Debra Webb is the award-winning *USA TODAY* bestselling author of more than one hundred novels, including those in reader-favorite series Faces of Evil, the Colby Agency and Shades of Death. With more than four million books sold in numerous languages and countries, Debra has a love of storytelling that goes back to her childhood on a farm in Alabama. Visit Debra at www.debrawebb.com.

Books by Debra Webb

Harlequin Intrigue

A Winchester, Tennessee Thriller

In Self Defense
The Dark Woods
The Stranger Next Door
The Safest Lies

Colby Agency: Sexi-ER

Finding the Edge
Sin and Bone
Body of Evidence

Faces of Evil

Dark Whispers
Still Waters

Colby Agency: The Specialists

Bridal Armor
Ready, Aim...I Do!

Colby, TX

Colby Law
High Noon
Colby Roundup

Debra Webb writing with Regan Black

Harlequin Intrigue

Colby Agency: Family Secrets

Gunning for the Groom

The Specialists: Heroes Next Door

The Hunk Next Door
Heart of a Hero
To Honor and To Protect
Her Undercover Defender

Visit the Author Profile page at Harlequin.com.

CAST OF CHARACTERS

Sadie Buchanan—No one is better at recovering a fellow agent who's in trouble. Sadie knows how to get in, recover the mark and get out. But this time is different. This time she's going in as a favor to a friend. The trouble is, she might not make it back out alive.

Smith Flynn—He's an enigma. A member of an extremist group who will stop at nothing to accomplish its mission. But every part of Sadie tells her this man is not who or what he seems.

Levi Winters—Sadie Buchanan has come to rescue him, but will she get them both killed trying?

Rayford Prentiss—The old man looks harmless, but looks can be deceiving.

Draven Aikman—He trusts no one and will do anything for what he wants.

Chapter One

Sadie Buchanan had never been to Winchester before. The closest she'd come was Tullahoma and that had been years ago when she was first assigned to the Nashville area. A joint task force conference at the Arnold Air Force base had required her attendance for a day. Frankly, it was unusual for an agent to end up in this area, much less request a retrieval. The kind of trouble that required her participation rarely happened in small towns. Most of her assignments took her to the larger metropolitan areas around the state or deep into the desert or the mountains.

In any event, whenever an agent was in trouble, she went in.

She parked in front of the Franklin County sheriff's office. Extracting agents from dangerous situations hadn't exactly been a part of her plan when she started her career, but within two years of her first field assignment she found herself doing exactly that after one particular mission. The assignment as well as the agent involved had been high profile, garnering her the full attention of the powers that be. During that fateful mission she as well as the Bureau discovered her knack for getting in and out with particular ease. From that point forward, she had been focused on training for moments like this one. It wasn't the sort of task just any agent felt comfortable doing. Success required a very particular skill set.

Go in, attain the target and get out alive.

Her father always said that everyone had a gift. Evidently, this was hers. It hadn't failed her yet. She had no intention of allowing it to start today.

Inside the brick building that housed the sheriff's department and county jail, a female desk sergeant greeted her.

"Special Agent Sadie Buchanan." Sadie showed her credentials to the other woman. "I'm here to see Sheriff Tanner and Agent Ross."

"Good morning, Agent Buchanan. Down the hall and to the left," Sergeant Rodriquez said with a gesture toward the long corridor beyond her desk. "They're waiting for you in the conference room, ma'am."

Sadie thanked the sergeant and headed in the direction she'd indicated. One thing she had noticed about Winchester already and it was barely ten o'clock in the morning—it was a couple of degrees hotter than Nashville. The town was attractive in a quaint sort of way, surrounded by a lake and bordered by hills and woods. Most folks would see those hills and woods as nature's perfect landscape. What Sadie saw in all that natural beauty were places to hide. Lots and lots of potential hiding places.

Not a good thing when attempting to locate a target.

She opened the door to the conference room and walked in. Four people waited for her but only one that she recognized: Special Agent Deacon Ross. He, too, was assigned to Nashville. They'd only worked together on one occasion, but he had a stellar reputation. The last she'd heard he had taken an extended leave of absence.

Maybe the rumors that he might not be coming back were just that—rumors. He certainly appeared to be involved in this case.

"Agent Buchanan," a tall, dark-haired man at the head of the table said as he stood, "I'm Sheriff Colt Tanner. We're glad you could come." He extended his hand.

Sadie gave his hand a shake. "Happy to help, Sheriff."

"This is Chief of Police Billy Brannigan." Tanner gestured to another man. This one had brown hair and eyes and looked as much like a cowboy as the sheriff.

Brannigan extended his hand across the conference table. "Good to meet you, Agent Buchanan."

"Likewise, Chief." Sadie accepted the gesture and turned to the next man in the room. "Agent Ross." She offered her hand.

Ross gave her hand a shake and then turned to the woman at his side. "This is Cecelia Winters."

Sadie extended her hand once more, this time toward the petite woman with the fiery mane of red hair. "Ms. Winters."

Winters brushed her palm briefly against Sadie's but didn't speak. Since she had the same last name as the target, Sadie assumed she was a wife or other family member.

"Why don't we have a seat and get started," Ross suggested.

Sadie pulled out a chair and sat down as the others resumed their seats. A couple of files and a stack of maps lay on the table. Not exactly the typical setup for a tactical mission briefing but she'd gotten the impression this one was different than her usual assignment. She didn't have a problem with different. As long as it didn't get anyone killed. Sadie was yet to lose a target once she had attained him or her.

"I imagine," Ross said, "you were briefed on the situation we have."

"I only just returned to Nashville late last night from an assignment in Memphis. I'm afraid the details I received are sketchy at best. I assumed I would be fully briefed when I arrived."

This would certainly be her first briefing with a civilian present who was totally unrelated to the official aspects of the investigation. She had a feeling this assignment was going to become more and more unusual.

"A particular group of extremists in the Franklin County area was pinpointed more than two decades ago. Gunrunning was suspected to be a major part of this group's activities. Over the past few years suspicions of their involvement with kidnapping, possibly related to human trafficking, have surfaced. My former partner, Jack Kemp, investigated this group when it was first discovered but at the time there was not enough substantial evidence that the members were involved in anything criminal or illegal to pursue any sort of operation. Just over nine years ago that status changed, and Jack came back for a second look. During the course of that assignment he disappeared. Recently, new information about what happened to him has come to light. In part, that information was obtained through a civilian informant. Like most of us, Jack worked with a number of civilian informants."

"One of those informants is Levi Winters," Sheriff Tanner added. "Levi has recently gone missing and we suspect this group may be involved."

Brannigan didn't add anything. Sadie was undecided as to whether his continued silence was a good thing. Perhaps his involvement was only for informational purposes. The target was likely outside his official jurisdiction.

"Is the Bureau opening a new case in the area?"

Seemed a no-brainer. But Sadie was not up to speed on the happenings in Franklin County. The more Ross talked, the more she understood that he had friends in high places and that was why she was here. "Or is this one off the record?"

The men in the room exchanged a look, which answered the question without anyone having to say a word.

"To a degree," Ross admitted, "the retrieval is off the record. There appears to be some hesitation about reopening the case involving the group known as Resurrection. Personally, I think we're caught in the middle of a war between the Bureau and the ATF, leaving us blind. We're hoping any information Levi may have will help pull this all together. But," he qualified, "finding him is our primary goal."

Making it doubly important that she brought him back alive. Sadie considered the other woman at the table. The hope in her eyes was impossible to miss. Right now, Sadie could walk away and that decision would not adversely affect her career since this mission was off the record. She could stand up, walk out that door and never look back rather than risk her life for some informant whom she did not know and had no idea if he was actually credible.

Chances were, if she made that decision, the informant would die.

And though that decision would not prove unfavorable to her career, it would prove immensely unfavorable to her conscience.

"Let's have a look at what I'm up against."

Tanner went first. He explained that he had not encountered any trouble with members of this group—at least none of which he was aware. The members of the so-called Resurrection group were anonymous. Any who lived amid the community kept quiet about their involvement. Neighbors, friends, possibly even family had no idea about their participation. The tactic was actually fairly common and had been used for centuries by one secret group or another.

Brannigan spoke for the first time, agreeing with Tanner's summation. The Winchester Police Department had not run into trouble with anyone who claimed to be or who was thought to be involved with this extremist group. The crime rate in the county was comparatively low. Rumors regarding the group known as Resurrection leaned toward the idea of extreme or doomsday-type preppers. Part of the problem was that there appeared to be an offshoot fringe group known only as the *others* who were far more dangerous. More primitive and violent.

Ross took over from there. "We've contacted a source within the ATF but we don't have anything back from him just yet. He can only help us so much without crossing a line. Whatever else we do, we can't keep waiting and risk losing Winters. Ultimately, the hope is that the Bureau and the ATF will initiate a joint task force, along with local law enforcement, to look more thoroughly into what this group is doing. As I said, for now, our immediate focus is on extracting Winters."

Sadie understood perfectly. "If the Resurrection or this offshoot group has him, we need to get their attention. Obviously—" she scanned the faces at the table "—you don't have the location where he's being held."

Tanner tapped the stacks of maps. "There are certain areas we feel are the more likely places but, no, we don't have a damned clue."

"And there's no time to conduct the kind of search required to locate a needle in a haystack," Sadie suggested. "Time is our enemy." She set her gaze on Ross's, knowing he would understand the goal. "We need their attention. I would recommend a news bulletin about a missing federal agent last seen in the Winchester area. Keep it ambiguous for obvious reasons. Give my description but not my name." She shifted her attention to Tanner. "I'll start with the most likely place and beat the bushes until they find me."

"You want them to find you?" Tanner looked uneasy as he asked the question.

"We don't have time to locate and infiltrate any other way. Prompting them to find me will be much faster and far more efficient."

"Isn't that far more dangerous, as well?" Brannigan asked.

"Yes." Sadie saw no point in whitewashing the answer. "But it's the only way to accomplish our goal in a timely manner."

"Agent Buchanan is highly trained for exactly these sorts of situations," Ross assured all present.

Judging by the expressions Tanner and Brannigan wore, his assurance did little to alleviate their reservations.

"You're suggesting going in without backup," Brannigan argued. "The only thing I see coming of that is two hostages needing extraction."

Sadie acknowledged his assessment with a nod. "That is a possibility. But, Chief, you can trust me when I say, if I wasn't experienced and completely confident about this situation, we wouldn't be having this conversation. I know what I'm doing. I understand the risk and, based on what I've heard so far, I am not overly concerned."

"I may be able to help."

All gathered around the table turned to the woman who had spoken. Cecelia Winters looked directly at Sadie even as the men in the room started to argue with her announcement.

"Not happening," Ross stated unconditionally, tension in his voice, his posture and the set of his jaw.

"He's right," Tanner agreed with a firm shake of his head.

"This whole thing is far too risky as it is," Brannigan added.

Sadie ignored them all. Instead, she focused on

the woman who had made the statement. "How do you believe you can help?"

Cecelia blinked at Sadie's question. "The people in this town know me. They know what happened to me—to my family. Nothing is secret anymore. If I spread the news, they'll believe me. They will pass it along far more quickly than something reported in the news. Not everyone around here trusts the news."

"Cece," Ross argued, "your getting involved could only complicate matters."

Sadie got the picture now. Ross and Cecelia were a couple. He didn't want her anywhere near the line of fire. A personal connection more often than not spelled trouble when it came to an assignment like this one.

"Help from most any source can be useful, but Ross could be right," Sadie said, not to change the woman's mind but because it was true.

The hard look Ross sent her way shouted loud and clear that he wasn't happy with how she had responded to the offer. Too bad. He wanted Sadie to do a job, an extraction—a very risky extraction. Why wouldn't she use any available resources?

"Levi is my brother," Cecelia said. "I want to help." She glanced at Ross. "I need to help."

"You understand that when this is over, there could be a backlash?" Sadie needed her to comprehend the long-term ramifications of any step she might opt to take. Sadie didn't like getting civilians involved but it seemed as if this one was already eye-ball deep in the situation.

"I do. The past decade of my life has been one long backlash. I think I can handle a little more."

Ross obviously didn't think so.

Sadie stared directly at him. "Is this going to be a problem for you?"

She didn't like problems. Especially those that came from the people who were supposed to be on her side.

He held her gaze for a moment before saying, "I guess not."

"Good." Sadie turned back to Cecelia. "You tell whomever you believe will get the word out the fastest that the agent who was working with your brother showed up and was going around town asking questions." She shrugged. "Trying to help, but now she's suddenly gone missing and you're worried about her."

Cecelia nodded. "I can do that."

"The most likely starting place?" Sadie asked, looking from one man to the next.

"The church," Ross said. He glanced at Cecelia as he spoke. "We have reason to believe the Salvation Survivalists were working with the primary group in some capacity. They were housing weapons most likely intended for the Resurrection group, but we don't have solid evidence of that conclusion. The ATF is looking at that aspect along with numerous others but, as we've established, they're taking too damned long and they're not sharing."

"But you're certain the two are or were connected."

"We are," Ross said.

Tanner and Brannigan agreed, as well.

"Then that's where I'll start." To Cecelia she said, "You put the word out about me asking questions." She shifted her attention to Tanner. "Make sure the local news reports a missing federal agent. No name, just a description," she reminded.

Tanner nodded. "I can make that happen."

"I'd like to familiarize myself with maps of the area, particularly around the church."

Ross spread the maps on the conference table and started the briefing regarding landscape. Sadie took her time and carefully committed the maps to memory. One of the things that made her good at her job was her ability to memorize maps and recall landmarks. For a girl who grew up in the city, she was a damned good tracker. As good as any hunter she'd ever worked with and she'd worked with a few.

More than anything, she paid attention. The old saying that it was all in the details was more often true than not. The details were crucial. One didn't need a photographic memory to recall the details. She just had to pay attention.

"What about the church?" Sadie considered the map of the area around the church, which appeared to be well outside town. "I need some additional history on the church."

"My father started the church about thirty-five years ago," Cecelia explained. "He was a very cruel man, capable of anything. He had many devoted followers who turned to my older brother, Marcus, after our father's murder. There are those who still believe one or both to be messiahs of a sort. I'm confident the most deeply devoted know far more than they've shared. If they hear about you, you better believe the word will go where you want it."

Ross pushed a folder in Sadie's direction. "This will give you a good overview of what we know. It's not complete by any means, but it's as much as anyone knows."

Sadie opened the file and skimmed the first page. "I'd like some time to go over what you have and then I'll drive out to the church, hide my car and start digging around. If I'm lucky, someone will come looking for me in short order."

"For the record," Chief of Police Brannigan spoke up again, "I still think this is a bad idea."

Sadie wished she could convince him otherwise but to an extent he was correct. This was most likely a bad idea.

But their options were limited. Sometimes the bad ideas were the only feasible ones.

Chapter Two

Dusk was settling way too fast. Sadie had knocked on doors in the vicinity of the church—not that there were that many. She'd asked straightforward questions, calling the group she sought by name. Then she'd driven to the now-defunct church of the Salvation Survivalists and she'd started poking around.

Breaking in had been a breeze. The ATF and the FBI had gone through the building numerous times and though every entrance had been secured, the lock on the back door was damaged. All of ten seconds were required to rip the crime scene seal away and finagle the thing open. As easy as taking candy from a baby.

It was possible a couple of days might be required to garner the attention she sought. Not good for her target. Levi Winters might not have a couple of days. On the other hand, it was possible he wasn't a hostage at all and was happily ensconced among friends deep within this suspicious group. His sister, Cecelia, was convinced he was a hostage, but sisters didn't always know the whole story.

Sadie's sister certainly did not.

She and her sister had never been friends. Maybe it was the ten years that separated them in age or the fact that her sister had chosen a path Sadie despised. Pricilla Buchanan was a criminal defense attorney. Her entire existence was focused on undoing what law enforcement personnel like Sadie risked their lives to do. Of course their mother insisted they were both angels, but she was wrong. Their mother wanted to see good in everyone. Pricilla was not good. She was self-centered, self-serving and indifferent when it came to justice.

Sadie kicked aside thoughts of her older sister as she strolled the halls of the extremist church whose followers still refused to speak ill of their most recent infamous leader. The man, Cecelia Winters's older brother as it turned out, had been hiding smuggled guns. He'd sworn he had no idea how the weapons had ended up in the secret underground hiding place beneath the church. He'd gone so far as to attempt to claim the weapons had been there since before his father died almost nine years ago. Talk about a scumbag. Then again, apparently his father had been an even bigger lowlife.

Ross and the others suspected Marcus Winters had been holding the stockpile of weapons for the Resurrection. Despite the seriousness of the charges he faced, Winters refused to spill his guts. Whomever Marcus Winters was protecting he was too damned afraid to make a deal, even for the promise of a new life in witness protection.

The moment he'd been arrested he had shut down like a dying cell phone battery and hadn't spoken since.

Anything that might provide clues about a connection between the church and the gunrunning extremist prepper group was long gone. The tunnel between the church and the Winters home was set for demolition. Cecelia mentioned that she intended to sell the place the moment it was released from evidence. She wanted to wash her hands of that ugly past as soon as possible and who could blame her? Based on what Ross had told Sadie, the woman had already paid a high price for standing up against her family.

Sadie followed the directions she'd been given to find the tunnel area. Mostly she was killing time. The longer she hung out in the area the more likely she was to run into what she was looking for. At least that was the hope. If she were really lucky things would happen as quickly as she hoped.

Ross had given her a piece of information to use as leverage once she had infiltrated the group. His contact from the ATF insisted this would be immensely useful. She'd gone into missions with less, but this felt a little slim by any measure.

The entrance to the tunnel was barricaded. Sadie turned and headed back in the direction she'd come.

She took the stairs two at a time and returned to the church's main sanctuary.

There was nothing else to be done here. She turned for the front entrance and stalled. A man sat on the very back pew. His hair was gray—not the white gray, the silver gray. It poked from beneath a fedora. A full beard did a hell of a job of camouflaging his face. He wore overalls and a button-down, long-sleeved shirt, no matter that it was as hot as hell outside. It was difficult to assess if he was armed. Her view of him from the chest down was blocked by the back of the pew in front of him. From a merely visual perspective he appeared reasonably harmless.

Sadie, however, was too smart to assume any such thing based on appearances.

"You must be that missing fed."

Though he said this in a low, rusty-with-age voice, it seemed to echo in the hollow sanctuary. Not particularly threatening and yet with simmering power.

"That's me. Sadie Buchanan."

"I hear you and a fed friend of yours have been looking for me."

Obviously, he meant Deacon Ross. "I don't know about anyone else and I definitely don't have any friends around here, but I've been looking for someone. That's a fact. Can't say whether that someone is you."

She dared to walk toward him, one step at a time down that long center aisle. The rubber soles of her hiking boots were quiet on the wood floor.

"What is it you think you're looking for, Ms. Buchanan? Or should I call you Agent Buchanan?"

Sadie sat down at the pew in front of him, turned in the hard seat to face him. "Sadie is fine. After yesterday, I doubt that anyone considers me an agent anymore—except maybe for the purposes of prosecution."

The story that she was an agent on the run was the best cover she could come up with given the circumstances and the shortness of time.

"Nine years. Stellar record. Up for promotion," he said, his gaze steady on hers, "the way I hear it. That's a lot to give up for whatever it is that brought you here, Sadie."

So the man had friends in the right places. Only a handful of people in this town knew her name and none beyond the four with whom she had met in the sheriff's conference room were aware of her background. She shrugged. "I should have gotten that promotion two years ago. And you're right, nine years is a long time to watch men like my SAIC write his own definition of justice. Besides, my daddy was a firm believer in a man—or woman—having the right to live his life the way he wanted and to bear arms. I suppose I have him to thank for my hardheadedness."

The man's gaze hardened. "As interesting as this conversation might prove to be, I don't like wasting my time, Sadie. Why don't you tell me what it is you think I need to hear?"

"I appreciate that you looked me up, Mister...?"

"Prentiss," he said, "Rayford Prentiss."

"Mr. Prentiss," she acknowledged. "The trouble is—and I mean no offense to you—I really need to speak with the man in charge. It's urgent. We don't have a lot of time."

He held her gaze for a long moment of thickening silence. "You don't look like the sort with a death wish," he finally said.

Sadie smiled. "Not if I can help it. What I have, Mr. Prentiss, is some information about a joint task force mission that will prove more than a little devastating to the Resurrection. If you and your friends take me in, I'll give you the heads-up you need to survive the storm that's coming—assuming you know what I'm talking about and have the authority to take me where I need to go."

A crooked smile lifted one corner of his bearded mouth. "First, I know precisely what you mean and I have all the authority I need. The real question is, why on God's green earth would I believe that foolish story?"

"Well, my motive is somewhat personal, Mr. Prentiss. I will tell you that I've gotten myself into a bit of trouble and I don't see any ready way out, so this looks like as good an option as any other. My daddy always said planning for the future was smart business. I need to disappear for a little while, Mr. Prentiss. I think you and your friends can make that happen. You do me a favor and I'll do one for you."

Prentiss chuckled. "I really am flummoxed, Sadie. You appear quite sincere and yet I'm not certain I believe you. Be that as it may, we'll play your little game. After all, it took considerable courage to start this thing." His gaze settled heavily on her and this time there was no mistaking the promise there. "Rest assured, whatever this is, if you're lying to me, you will not like how this ends."

"Great." Sadie pushed a smile into place and sat up straight. "Then we have a deal."

Another of those long moments of silence elapsed with him staring at her. "It appears we do."

He raised a hand and people seemed to come out of the woodwork. Four men, all armed. "My friends will see to your transportation. Goodbye, Sadie."

When he stood and walked away, she couldn't help wondering if this mission would end right here, right now. These guys could kill her and no one would ever know exactly what happened, much less who did the deed.

Wasn't that the way it always was?

The door closed behind Prentiss and she stood, glanced from fierce face to fierce face. "So, who's driving?"

"Take off your clothes," the one nearest her said.

She laughed. "I never take off my clothes on the first date."

He aimed his weapon at her. "Take them off now."

One of his pals stepped forward and tossed a bag on the floor at the end of her pew.

"There are clothes in the bag," the one who appeared to be in charge and who held his aim steady on her announced.

"Well, if you insist."

Taking her time she toed off her boots, peeled off her socks, then unbuttoned her shirt. When the shirt, the boots and socks were in a neat pile next to the provided bag, she shucked her jeans and added them to the pile next.

When she reached for the bag, the man with the gun at the ready protested, "Everything comes off."

She figured that would be his next order. Sadie reached behind her and unhooked her bra. She allowed it to fall forward and drop to the pile. Then she swooped off her panties and added them unceremoniously to the rest.

The man nodded and she reached for the bag. Inside was a pair of gray sweatpants and a white tee. No underwear. No socks. Thankfully there was a pair of plastic flip-flops. The cheap kind found in bins near the checkout counter at discount stores. She donned the provided outfit and slipped her feet into the flip-flops.

The man who'd brought the bag grabbed her things and put them into the empty bag. She hated that her cell phone was in that bag. Besides a gun, it was the asset she depended upon most.

Oh well.

"Let's go." The man with a bead on her motioned

with the barrel of his weapon toward the back of the church.

"What about my car?" she asked as they marched toward the rear exit.

"A friend will pick it up and dismantle it for parts."

She stalled and glared at the man. Was he out of his mind? "Wait just a minute. That car cost—"

"You won't need it where you're going."

THE DRIVE TO their destination took half an hour, give or take a minute.

Sadie had counted off the seconds and minutes, in part to distract herself from the sorts of thoughts that wanted to crowd into her brain. But mostly because it was important to maintain a sense of location. Half an hour from the church was a reference anyone coming to her rescue could use to facilitate the task.

Except there was no one coming. This mission was basically off the books. Ross and his friends would get worried when they didn't hear from her in a couple of days but there wasn't a whole lot they could do other than beat the bushes and rattle a few cages looking for her. Finding her would be difficult if not impossible. The tracking devices in her cell phone, in the soles of her shoes and in her bra were who knew where. Unless someone had been watching her and followed this caravan, she was probably out of luck as far as backup was concerned.

Frankly, she had been surprised by their vehicles. She'd expected big four-wheel-drive trucks caked with mud and decked out with gun racks. But that wasn't the case at all. The two vehicles were both new top-of-the-line SUVs. Sure, they were four-wheel drive, but they were sleek and almost elegant looking—unlike the men inside.

The younger of the group had been tasked with her personal security. He'd secured her hands behind her back and dropped a cloth bag over her head. He sat in the back seat with her. Another one drove. The other two men were in the second vehicle, with Prentiss, no doubt. No one in this vehicle had said a word en route. Music had played just loud enough to prevent her from noting another reference—any sounds in the areas they drove through. Animals, trains, construction, whatever.

When the vehicle rolled to a stop and the engine cut off, the music died. The doors opened and low voices rumbled around her. Beyond the voices was quiet. No city sounds. No traffic sounds. Not even any animals.

Fingers wrapped around her upper arm and tugged her from the center section of the back seat. A hand guided her feet so she wouldn't break her neck climbing out. When she was steady on the ground the sack was dragged from her head.

Her first thought was that she had gone back in time. The towering stone walls made her think of the ones surrounding a castle she'd visited in Edinburgh,

Scotland. The walls were massive, at least thirty feet high. There were what appeared to be guard towers built into the wall. A large, square stone structure stood in the center of the expansive grounds that were like a quad on a college campus without all the fancy landscape. Like the primitive keeps she'd seen in her travels, the windows were tiny in proportion. There were other buildings beyond the larger one, but she could only see the rooftops in the distance.

She stared overhead. Frowned. There was no sky.

She scanned what should have been the sky for as far as she could see. Steel and some sort of panels stood high above her. Reminded her of a massive warehouse. But no clouds or sun or anything else that said *sky*.

Wherever they were, they were not outside. But the SUVs had rolled to a stop right here. She glanced over her shoulder at the one she'd only just emerged from. The ride had seemed to stay on level ground. There had been no downhill or uphill movement. The ride had been smooth but not so smooth that she wouldn't have noticed a change in elevation. There could have been an elevator somewhere that brought them below ground. But that didn't seem right, either, since they hadn't stopped long enough to roll into any sort of elevator until a minute ago, when the engines shut off and they got out.

The man behind her nudged her forward with the muzzle of his weapon. She took in as much of what she could see as possible, committed it to memory as they moved forward. Wherever they were, the place was certainly fortified for battle. If they were underground as she suspected, she supposed the purpose was for surviving a nuclear attack. Additionally, being underground would explain why the feds and local law enforcement hadn't already spotted the compound from the air.

By the time they rounded the corner of the largest building she'd seen so far, only two of the men remained with her. Prentiss and the other two had gone in a different direction. The one with the gun at her back kept her moving forward with the occasional nudge. Beyond the large building were increasingly smaller ones. Along the east side of the wall the smallest structures were numbered. They sat in a long row like cabin rentals at the lake. Only there was no lake—not that she'd seen so far anyway—and this was no vacation. The long, low building that stood the farthest west from the center of the grounds had no windows and appeared to be their destination. The squat roofline told her it was one story. She saw only one entrance along the front, assuming what she was looking at was the front.

The second of the two guards unlocked and opened the door. Number one nudged her to go in. The guards followed close behind her. An immediate left took them down a long white corridor lined with doors on either side. No windows on the doors, either. Midway down the corridor, they stopped at a door and number two guard unlocked it with a few clicks of the keys on the control pad. Once the thick door pulled outward, Sadie understood this would be her accommodations for now. Until they decided what to do with her, she imagined.

"I'm supposed to be meeting with the man in charge," she reminded number one.

"Tomorrow."

The door slammed in her face.

She turned around. A dim light came from around the perimeter of the room. There was a steel cot, a toilet hanging on the wall with a sink formed in the tank. Just like the ones she had seen in the few prison cells she'd visited.

With a quick drawing back of the covers, she checked the mattress, ensured the sheets weren't tainted with anything she could see or smell. Fabric smelled clean enough. She paced the small room and considered her options. There had been four men with Prentiss. She hadn't seen any others when they arrived but that didn't mean there weren't hundreds around here somewhere. There was no accurate body count for this group.

If the Resurrection was like most of these extremist groups, there would be several hundred on-site. This was obviously a headquarters. The setup was too good to be anything else. The Bureau had been gathering information on extremist groups like this for decades. But this one had somehow managed to stay under the radar. The members didn't talk. Fear, she imagined. It was human nature to talk about the things in which one was interested. Being a part of something like Resurrection would typically provide bragging rights for those who had a penchant for the extreme. But there was no bragging from these members.

Their silence made them even more dangerous. Restricted the available intelligence to gather, making the jobs of Sadie and others like her far more difficult. Law enforcement personnel depended upon informants and the information garnered on the streets. When information stopped flowing, it was impossible to find footing in a given situation.

Sadie braced her hands on her hips and moved around the room again, this time more slowly. She considered the walls, thought about the door when it had opened. The walls were likely made of concrete just as the door was. Thick concrete, eight inches at least. The floor and ceiling of this building appeared to be the same as the walls. The smooth, cold finish of the concrete was interrupted only by the small blocks of light around the walls near the floor. The cot was metal, the sheets a thin material more like paper than fabric. No good for constructing a hangman's noose. She turned back to the door. The lock wasn't the usual residential sort. It was electronic and required a code.

Getting out of here wouldn't be easy. If she was really lucky, Levi Winters was in this same building. Assuming he was a hostage. Hopefully, he would know a way out and would be willing to go with her.

That was the problem with being underground or, perhaps, burrowed into a mountainside. Getting out was generally somewhat complicated.

She'd been in tighter spots, Sadie reminded herself.

All she had to do was find her target and she would locate a way out of here.

It was what she did.

Chapter Three

The woman was trouble.

Smith Flynn studied the screen monitoring her movements. She paced the six-by-eight cell as if the journey might end some other way the next time she turned around. She hadn't stopped since being placed inside. This restless behavior was for the benefit of anyone observing.

He had watched her arrival. She had walked into the compound, shoulders back, chin held high, all the while discreetly surveying everything in her field of vision. Sadie Buchanan was neither afraid nor uncertain. Her arrival at this compound was not by accident any more than was the timing of her appearance. She was on a mission.

Whatever she was doing here, unfortunately she was his issue now.

He did not like unexpected issues. Even fearless, attractive ones like Sadie Buchanan.

"What's your take on this new development?"

The voice drew Smith from his musings. He

turned to Prentiss. The older man had been running the group known as the Resurrection for a very long time. He rarely had much to say but when he spoke anyone within hearing distance listened—not because he was so articulate or interesting, but because they wanted to live. Prentiss did not take disrespect well.

"She has an agenda," Smith said, not telling the other man anything he didn't already know. "It'll take some time to determine what that agenda is."

Prentiss nodded, his attention fixed on the screen. "I don't like killing women. There's something innately wrong with a man killing a woman. It's a sin like no other, except for killing a child. Any man who would kill a woman or a child is lower than low." His gaze swung to Smith. "But, if you tell me she's lying, I will kill her."

Smith didn't waste time pretending to consider the situation. "I can tell you right now that she *is* lying. No question there." He turned his attention back to the screen. "The question is why. We'll need that answer before you kill her."

Prentiss nodded. "You're right. Until we have the answer, she belongs to you. Do with her what you will, just get the truth for me."

"I always do."

The old man stood and headed for the door. Smith waited until the door closed before turning back to the screen. He wondered if this woman had any idea just how much trouble she was in. Whatever she thought she'd come here to do, she had made a most regrettable mistake.

He exited his cabin, locking the door behind him, and crossed to the detention center. No one questioned his movements. They knew better. The door was unlocked and opened for him as if he was a king. Once inside he said to the guard, "I'll be using interview room two for an hour or so. Bring me Levi Winters."

"Yes, sir."

The guard hustled away to do Smith's bidding. Smith took the short corridor on the right and then an immediate left where six interview rooms waited. Each room was equipped with very specific instruments for persuading answers from those who had the misfortune of ending up in one of the spaces. Before going to interview room two, he stepped into the observation room and checked the monitoring system.

Two minutes elapsed before the guard entered interview room two. He settled the prisoner Levi Winters into the chair on the side of the metal table facing the hidden camera. Once Winters was secured to the bolt in the concrete floor, the guard exited. Smith considered Winters for a longer moment. He was younger than this woman who'd gotten herself invited to this ultrasecure place.

More important than any other aspect of this prisoner, he was scared. Scared to death.

THEY WERE PROBABLY going to kill him now.

Levi's whole body felt as cold as ice. There was no telling what they had planned for him this time. That bastard Flynn had done things to him, made him talk when he didn't want to talk.

Levi closed his eyes and lowered his head. He was doomed. All he'd wanted was to find the truth. To prove to his sister that he wasn't a bad guy like their brother, Marcus. He'd let her down so badly already it hurt to think about it. Even under the circumstances. He hadn't helped Cece the way he should have so he'd decided to prove the whole truth about their daddy and all that he and Marcus had done, like ordering the death of the FBI guy, Jack Kemp.

Jack had been good to Levi. He'd made him feel like his life mattered—like he mattered. Levi had wanted to be like him. And then the guy had disappeared.

What nobody knew was that Levi remembered the night their mother had died, no matter that he'd been nothing but a little kid. She and that bastard who was their father had been arguing so loudly and so desperately—arguing, screaming and crying. Then suddenly the arguing had stopped. Levi had crept out of his bedroom and to the top of the stairs. Their momma had lain at the bottom of the stairs. The crying had started again, only that time it was

Levi. The only thing he remembered after that was Cece holding him and their grandmother screaming. Eventually she had calmed down and taken them home with her.

The certainty and hatred that had sprouted that night had grown and grown but before Levi could work up the courage to do what needed to be done, their younger sister, Sierra, had killed the old bastard. It should have been Levi. He should have killed that devil and taken care of the family when their older brother, Marcus, had not. But Levi had been weak. He'd been weak and afraid. He'd let Cece down and now he was going to die without having made up for the past.

He wished he could see Cece one more time and tell her how sorry he was. She had paid the price for all of them.

The door opened and Levi froze. It would be him—the one the other prisoners called the Interrogator. Levi's body shuddered at the idea of what he might have planned for him this time. Why had he screwed up so badly yet again? All he wanted at this point was to go home. To show his sister how much he loved her and to start doing the right thing with his life.

He wasn't like his father or his older brother. Evil didn't swim in his blood.

He just wanted to go home.

Smith Flynn walked into the room. He had the lightest gray eyes, almost transparent. That and his

blond hair almost made him look like some guy from
Norway or Sweden or something. He didn't look like
anyone from around here. He was tall, six-four at
least. And strong. You could tell he pumped iron.
But he hadn't laid a hand on Levi. He had other ways
to induce pain. He used equipment and his words.
He knew the things to say to strike terror in a man.

Before Levi could stop himself, his gaze flitted
to the far end of the room where the metal cabinets
stood. Inside those locked doors were instruments he
hoped to never see again. Evidently he wasn't going
to be so lucky. Flynn wouldn't be here otherwise.

The worst part about the whole damned mess was
that this guy wanted some truth from Levi, but he
didn't have anything to trade for his life or even for
a little more time free of torture. Levi had nothing.
He had come to this place to prove something. All
those years ago when he'd first joined the Resurrection so Jack Kemp would see how smart he was, he'd
made a mistake. Truth was he'd let Jack use him.
He'd needed that father figure Jack represented so
badly. Levi would have done anything to impress
him. But he'd gone too far.

All he'd done was gotten into trouble. Now he
was likely going to get dead the same way Jack had.

Levi would end up in hell with his damned daddy.

"We have a new problem, Levi."

Fear tightened around his neck. Even the man's
voice had a way of terrifying anyone who happened
to be stuck in the room with him. Deep, dark, dan-

gerous. Fear twisted inside Levi. Why didn't this Interrogator just kill him and get it over with? He didn't want to die but he couldn't take this much longer.

"I already told you I don't know anything. I only came here to find the truth about an old friend. I swear that's it. The whole story. The truth. There's nothing else."

"Jack Kemp," Flynn said. "You told me that before. Tell me again why you think Kemp came here?"

"He was from the FBI," Levi said. No point pretending he could hide anything from this bastard. The Interrogator had ways of digging stuff out of him. "He asked me to help him get information about the group called the Resurrection, but I went too far."

"Meaning you joined the calling all those years ago? Nine or so years ago, am I right? You did this to help your friend."

Levi nodded. "But Jack disappeared before I could tell him anything. I figured y'all found out what he was up to and got rid of him."

"Your brother, Marcus, was responsible for what happened to him, Levi. If you had seen the news recently, you would know this. He confessed."

Levi was surprised that Marcus confessed to giving Jack to those crazy people. The only way he would have admitted to anything was to save his sorry ass. Hurt twisted in Levi's chest. "What about my sisters? Did you see anything about my sisters?"

Flynn directed that icy glare at him. "Do I look like I would waste my time keeping up with your sisters?"

Levi blinked, bit his tongue so hard he tasted blood. He wanted to hurt this guy. But he'd heard all about him—the Interrogator. The one who got the answers for the Council. The one who knew how to cause pain. Fear snaked through Levi. He shouldn't have come back here. He'd wanted to help...but he'd just made another mistake. Jack was dead by now, no question. Marcus was in jail. God only knew about Sierra. Hopefully Cece was okay.

Flynn placed a photo of a woman on the table. "Do you know her?"

The woman had black hair and eyes nearly as dark, like a raven. Her skin was dark, like she'd lain on a beach all summer. She was pretty but he hadn't seen her before. He shook his head. Prayed that was the right answer because it was the only one he had. "No. She doesn't look familiar."

"Are you certain? Think carefully, Levi. If you lie to me, it will be much worse for you."

"I swear to God I don't know the woman. I have never seen her before."

Flynn said nothing for a long moment. Levi's chest felt ready to explode with tension. Why the hell didn't the bastard just go ahead and tell him he was a dead man? If death was coming, he'd rather know now and brace for it. He was sick of these games. He did not know this woman. He did not know any other information related to the FBI or this damned place or any damned thing else that mattered. His foot started to bounce, making his shackles rattle.

He forced himself to still. Losing it wouldn't help his situation.

"I believe you, Levi." Flynn withdrew the photo, tucked it away in a folder. "My true concern is that she appeared here only a few days after you."

Agony welled inside Levi. "I don't know why. I don't know her. Why don't you ask her?"

"Not to worry, I certainly will. I think I might know why she's here but I need to be certain."

Levi blinked. He didn't have a damned clue where this was going or what this woman had to do with him. He just wanted to go back to his cell and be left alone. He didn't want the Interrogator opening up those cabinets over there the way he'd done before. Pulling out his torture tools and making Levi nearly piss his pants.

Ever since he was a teenager, Levi had thought that to some degree he was brave. He'd thought he was the kind of man who did the right thing. A sort of hero. At least he'd wanted to be. He'd hoped he could be a hero for his sister Cece and help her prove her innocence…but he hadn't helped. And he damned sure wasn't a hero. He wasn't even brave.

He was a coward.

Nothing but a stinking coward.

"Can I count on your help, Levi?"

Levi snapped his focus back to the man. He swallowed back the bile that had risen in his throat and tried to slow his pounding heart. "Yeah, sure. What do I have to do?"

"I haven't worked out all the details just yet. We'll talk again soon."

The man stood and walked out.

Levi sagged in his chair. Squeezed his eyes shut and thanked God he'd survived a second encounter with the Interrogator.

Whatever he wanted, Levi could do it. He would do it. At this point obedience was probably the only way to stay alive. Cece would want him to stay alive. She would. He knew this without question. His sister would absolutely want him to do whatever necessary to stay alive.

Even if he was the worst kind of coward.

SMITH RETURNED TO his cabin and turned on the security feed to watch the woman.

She had stopped her pacing. Had decided to conserve her energy. He suspected she was above average in intelligence. Certainly she was cockier than the average agent. Her dark hair and eyes, the olive skin, gave her an exotic appearance. Beyond the superficial, she looked strong. Undeniable curves, but not soft. Lean. Toned muscle. This was a woman who worked hard to be prepared.

Her claim of possessing useful information was not a particularly original tactic. Her methods of getting their attention, however, were damned original. To garner the attention of Prentiss himself, then get herself picked up by members and brought here this way was ingenious. And extremely risky. Whatever she wanted, it was important. Important enough to risk her life.

Reconnaissance teams had been doubled and were out there now, patrolling and watching for trouble. No matter that the team that had brought her here had ensured they weren't followed. Her clothes and personal items had been removed before she left that godforsaken church. That level of motivation demanded careful consideration.

It was possible a tracking device was implanted somewhere on her slim body but the initial scan had not picked up on anything close to the surface. Her clothes and cell phone had been cleaned. As he'd anticipated, her phone was more or less a blank slate. Anything incriminating had been wiped. It had been reduced to a mere tracking device. This was a very well-trained agent.

Rather than take the risk the initial scan had missed something, he picked up a secure internal line and called Medical. "Run deep scans on Prisoner Buchanan. Send the results to me ASAP."

Smith ended the call, his attention still focused on the woman. He watched as she whirled around at the sound of her cell door opening. She didn't resist when the guard cuffed her hands behind her back and then escorted her out of the confining space. Smith followed the monitors, watching her move down the long white corridor and out onto the quad. The two crossed the common area and entered the smaller medical building. Smith switched to another camera and followed their movements inside.

The guard took a position at the door leading to Imaging while the waiting technician assumed custody of the prisoner.

"Remove your clothing," the tech ordered.

Buchanan glanced around the room, noted the imaging equipment and then did as he asked without question. The top came off first, revealing high, firm breasts and a narrow waist. As the sweatpants slid down her hips and thighs, Smith's gaze followed. Despite his own training, his body tightened. Her shape was undeniably attractive. Gently rounded hips and long legs sculpted by hours of running. Her long hair hung around her shoulders, the only remaining shield she possessed.

The quality he found most surprising and interesting was that she stared square at the male technician without the slightest flinch. She was not shy or afraid.

Smith continued to observe as the scans were accomplished. On a second screen, he monitored the results. There was no indication a tracking device or other electronic object had been inserted or implanted. She was clean.

His curiosity roused. This woman—this Federal Bureau of Investigation agent—had walked into a compound filled with heavily armed and well-trained extremists. In truth, the people here were more mercenaries than preppers. She had done this while completely unarmed and with no way to call for backup or hope to escape.

Sadie Buchanan was either telling the truth about her agenda for being here or she was completely insane.

He would know the answer soon enough.

Chapter Four

Saturday, August 4

Sadie opened her eyes. Darkness crowded in around her, jolting her heart into a frantic run.

For a moment her brain couldn't assimilate where she was. Air refused to fill her lungs.

Then she remembered. Compound. *Resurrection.* Trouble.

She froze.

What had awakened her so abruptly? A sound. The slightest brushing of fabric against fabric as if someone had come far too close to her huddled position on this rock-hard cot.

She dared to take a breath and the subtle scent of leather and wood whispered against her senses. Adrenaline burned through her once more.

She was not alone.

Forcing herself to relax, she peered into the darkness. Slowly but surely her eyes filled in the dark form sitting on the edge of the thin mattress, barely centimeters away. Whoever it was sat perfectly still, didn't even breathe.

Someone had come into her cell, had walked the half-dozen steps across the small concrete room and sat down on the edge of her cot. The door opening should have awakened her but it had not. Had they put something into her food?

She never slept so heavily.

"What do you want?" She said the words then waited for a response, holding her breath for fear she would miss some part of the answer, assuming an answer came.

"Why are you here, Sadie Buchanan?"

Male. His voice was intensely deep, and...*dangerous*. She couldn't stop the shiver the sound elicited.

Grabbing back her usual unflappability, she fired back, "You already know the answer to that question."

A grunt was his immediate reaction.

She ordered herself to relax. Where was her usual fearlessness? It was something for which she didn't typically have to search. Granted he had startled her from sleep in the middle of the night. Then again, she couldn't be sure what time it was. It could be morning for all she knew. Without a window with which to judge, she couldn't make an accurate assessment. There had to be something in the food she had dared to nibble at. She had known better but hunger sometimes overrode experience.

"Why are you here, Sadie Buchanan?" he said once more.

The words were harsher this time. His patience was thinning, and he obviously didn't like repeating himself. Well, she didn't, either.

"Like I told your friends, I have information that could help your cause. I came to make a deal."

He laughed. There was zero humor in the rough noise. "If you were half as smart as you apparently believe you are, Sadie Buchanan, you would know that people like us don't make deals."

The full depth and breadth of her courage finally reared its head. About time. "Well, now, that's not entirely true, Mister…?"

"Flynn. Smith Flynn."

Her brain instinctively searched her memory banks. No Smith Flynn was found there. "Perhaps you're unaware of the deals those in charge make quite often. Deals with a certain South American gunrunning cartel. The recent shipment was detained by the feds and local authorities right here in Winchester—assuming we're still in the Winchester area. And that's only the beginning of your troubles. Things are not going to go so well for your friends if you refuse my generous offer of help."

He appeared to contemplate her warning for a time. If she was really lucky, his curiosity would trump his logic.

"What happened recently," he said, his voice still somehow disturbing to her senses, "was an unforeseeable stroke of good fortune for *your* friends, but it won't happen again."

Sadie was the one who laughed this time. "You really believe all those stored weapons were found in those underground tunnels at the church by accident? A lucky break for the feds?"

His tension shifted to the next level; she felt it in his posture even if she couldn't see him in the darkness. Though their bodies weren't touching, tension crackled between them. He was as edgy as she was. She squinted, peered harder through the darkness. Her eyes had adjusted more fully to the darkness allowing her to see that he had lighter hair. Blond, she calculated. Maybe gray. She couldn't say for certain.

"You have proof it wasn't?"

The next step was a risky one. Other than Levi Winters, she had no names of members except the one she was saving as the ace up her sleeve. "I know what the local authorities said. A heads-up took them to the church. The Winters family meltdown was secondary. They were already going there anyway. The church had been on their radar for a while. The goal was to hit when it counted. We both know how that turned out."

He considered her statement for long enough to make her doubt herself.

"I can't decide, Sadie Buchanan, whether you actually have relevant information or if you simply have a somewhat complicated death wish. If exiting this world is your goal, putting your service weapon to your temple would have been far easier."

"I can assure you, Mr. Flynn, I do not have a death wish." She was winning this round. "What I have is information you and your friends can use. But I can't force your interest." She relaxed into the thin mattress as if she'd said all she had to say.

"I will be watching you, Sadie Buchanan. If you're lying, you will regret your actions far more than you can imagine."

She reached out, her hand landing on what felt like his upper arm. The muscles there were like steel but she suspected that had nothing to do with him not being relaxed and everything to do with serious workouts.

"Tell me about you, Smith Flynn. What's your story? What are you running away from?"

He snagged her hand, clutched it in his own. "Why would you think I'm running from something?" His thumb found her palm and stroked the tender flesh there. "You don't know me."

His touch unnerved her, which was the point. "How can you be certain I don't know you? No one is invisible, Mr. Flynn."

The mattress shifted and fabric rustled as he leaned close. His face came so near to hers she could feel his breath on her skin. Her own ability to breathe stalled.

"I know this because you have never seen my face.

A name is only a name. It's the face—the eyes—that tell the story, and I will know yours."

With every ounce of courage she possessed, she forced herself to turn fully toward him, putting their mouths mere millimeters apart. "Then show me your face and we'll know for certain."

She felt his smile. "You are very brave, Sadie Buchanan. Or perhaps you are more naive than I thought."

"I thought you had me all figured out, Mr. Flynn."

"So did I."

He drew away and she dared to breathe again.

"You have a command performance this morning, Ms. Buchanan." The mattress shifted again as he stood. "I hope for your sake you pass the series of tests you are about to encounter. If some part of you recognizes that you're in over your head, you might consider quitting now. I'm confident the Council would be willing to permit a quick, merciful death if you confessed the truth before wasting more of their time."

"I'm not a quitter, Mr. Flynn." Sadie dropped her feet to the floor. "If you knew me at all, you would know this."

The next sound she heard was the door closing and then locking.

Just to be sure he was actually gone and not waiting in the darkness, she stood and moved around the walls of the room, reaching out to ensure he wasn't standing in the center of the dark space.

She leaned against the door and closed her eyes. He might be right about one thing—there was a very strong possibility she was in over her head.

THE GUARD USHERED her out the exit. This one, like the ones yesterday and the men who had accompanied Prentiss, wore a camouflage military uniform. The boots were military style, as well. Outside, Sadie squinted at the light. It seemed so bright she had to remind herself it wasn't the sun. There was no sky because this place was underground somehow.

"Where is this place?" she asked the man ushering her along. "Underground? In a cave?" If it was a cave, it was a really large cave. Maybe it was built into a mountainside. That would explain how they'd driven directly in and why the facility had not been located by any sort of aerial surveillance.

As usual, the man ushering her along said nothing. Even when he'd opened her cell a few minutes ago, he hadn't spoken. She had gotten up from the cot and walked out, grateful to escape the concrete box.

"If we're underground…" Sadie stopped, causing him to almost trip over her. "Technically I don't need these cuffs. Where would I go if I ran?"

He glared at her, grabbed her by the upper arm and steered her forward.

"Where are we going?"

Still not a word.

The smaller buildings, almost like cabins, captured her attention again. Living quarters for those in charge, she surmised. Somewhere around here there would be a barracks for those members like the one escorting her this morning. She wondered about the man who had come to her cell sometime during the night. He probably lived in one of those private quarters.

"Were you on duty all night?"

Still no answer. He walked forward, his gaze straight ahead.

"A man came into my cell." She almost stumbled trying to look back over her shoulder at the mute guard as she spoke. But she was glad she did. He made the slightest little flinch in response but quickly schooled his face. She couldn't decide if he'd felt a fleeting hint of concern that she might fall or if the idea of the man who visited her unsettled him somehow.

"He tried to scare me."

No reaction.

"But he didn't scare me. If he'd intended to kill me, he would have."

"There are worse things than dying."

His fingers wrapped around her upper arm once more and ushered her toward a building on the left. The sign posted by the door read Clinic. She wanted to question him about the comment, but he ushered her through the entrance and walked away before she could. A woman wearing a white uniform took charge of Sadie.

"The guard will wait for you outside," the nurse, doctor, whatever she was, explained.

The woman, her black hair slicked back in a tight bun, led the way to a plain white room with an exam table as well as a side table loaded with medical equipment. Sadie decided the woman was a nurse or technician. She checked Sadie's temperature and then led the way back into the corridor.

In the next room, there was yet another examination table. A stack of neatly folded sweatpants and a tee sat on the table. Beyond that was a curtain—the type that would hang over a shower.

The nurse pulled a key from her pocket and removed the cuffs, then gestured to the curtain. "Take off your clothes and shower. Use the soap in the bottle."

Sadie didn't argue. She took off her clothes, got into the shower and washed her hair and body as instructed. When she'd finished and stepped out of the shower, the woman—nurse, whatever she was—waited by the exam table. She wore an apron, a face mask and gloves. Stirrups now extended from one end of the table.

"We'll do your exam now."

No point in arguing. Sadie climbed onto the exam table and placed her feet in the stirrups. A close physical examination followed. She rolled Sadie onto her side and checked her back and buttocks. She scanned her arms and legs, hands and feet. Her face and scalp. Then she did a pelvic exam.

Sadie grimaced. "You looking for anything in particular?"

They had scanned her thoroughly yesterday. This seemed a bit overkill.

The woman peeled off her gloves and tossed them into a trash receptacle. "Put on your clothes."

Sadie complied. When the fresh sweats and tee hung on her body, the nurse recuffed her and led her back out the front entrance to where the guard waited. From there, he led Sadie toward yet another building, this one about the same size as the clinic. The sign on the door read Council. The building was like all the rest, gray, like concrete. Austere. This one was a one-story like the clinic and the detention center.

As soon as they stepped inside the building Sadie understood this was a place of importance. The floor was carpeted. Something commercial with low pile, but enough to quiet footsteps. The walls weren't a stark white as all the others had been. This was more of a beige.

"What did you mean when you said there were worse things than dying?"

"Wait here." He steered her toward the waiting bench. "Maybe you won't have to find out."

Sadie sat on the bench against the wall and watched as he walked away. She ignored the idea that he had a point about there being some things worse than dying. For now, she preferred to focus on more optimistic scenarios. She had a feeling she was on a dangerous precipice. Whatever happened in the next few minutes would determine her future. One slip either way and she could go over the edge completely.

Minutes passed. Three, then four and five. Eventually ten. Sadie crossed her legs, uncrossed them and then crossed them again. She swung her foot up and down. Someone in this place was watching her. She might as well show them how thoroughly unimpressed and utterly bored she was.

A door on the opposite side of the corridor, a few yards beyond where she sat, opened. A different guard—she recognized the camo uniform but not the face—strode to her, pulled her to her feet and shepherded her toward the door he'd exited. The room was fairly large. A long table stood across the far end; seven, no eight men were seated on the other side. One chair sat on this side of the table. Sadie suspected that chair was for her. The guard nudged her forward, confirming her suspicion. When she'd taken a seat, he waited behind her.

Most of the men were old and Caucasian. Not a particularly big surprise. There was one, however, who was not so old. A few years older than Sadie. Maybe forty. Blond hair. Piercing gray eyes. He stared at her, as did the others, but there was something about his stare that penetrated far deeper. They wore civilian clothes. Jeans, short-sleeved shirts—some button-down, others pullovers—and hiking boots. Except for one.

Of all those present, the only person among them

she had seen before was the man named Prentiss. He wore the same style overalls and long-sleeved shirt he'd worn in their first meeting. No fedora this time.

He spoke first. "Agent Buchanan, you've created quite a stir around here." He glanced side to side, acknowledging his colleagues. "We're mostly in agreement as to what should become of you. There's a single holdout, preventing a final decision."

Sadie made a face. "I'm not sure I understand, Mr. Prentiss. You haven't heard what I have to say. Maybe you're not interested in protecting your assets and followers."

He stared directly at her, his glare as deadly as any weapon she'd ever faced. "I don't think you understand, Agent Buchanan. We have no interest in anything you have to say. We have our doubts as to the worth of anything you might have to offer and we've decided we have no patience for whatever game you're playing."

Not exactly the reaction she'd hoped for. Time to throw out the ace up her sleeve. "Mr. Trenton Pollard." She scanned the faces as she said the name, looking for a reaction or some indication that one or more of those present recognized the name. Everyone seated at the table—except the younger man— had shoulder-length hair, a full beard and mustache, hiding a good portion of their faces, but not one of them outwardly flinched, grimaced or so much as batted an eye.

"The Bureau and the ATF," she went on, "have

targeted Resurrection with the intention of taking down those in power, starting with you, Mr. Prentiss. They consider you the weak link in this group. The necessary information to accomplish this feat will be provided by Mr. Pollard. It's my understanding there's more than simply your location, far more, he plans to share."

All eyes stared at her.

Good or bad, she'd shown her hand—her only hand. Now the ball was in their court.

She had nothing else.

Except what she could make up as she went along. She'd always been fairly good at improvising.

The men whispered among themselves, save the younger one. He sat staring at Sadie without saying a word or even glancing at anyone else. That he still watched her so closely had begun to get under her skin. She kept her attention on the others, hoping all that going back and forth was in her best interest.

Finally, a hush fell over the group and Prentiss settled his attention on her once more. "Agent Buchanan, we still have reservations about your decision to come here with this so-called warning. Though I will give you this, you have our attention. Still, my question to you is what could you possibly hope to gain?"

Now for the improvising. "I screwed up." She shrugged. "I had an opportunity to pad my bank account and I took it. I see no reason to share the dirty details. Sadly, two days ago I found out an investigation had been opened and my assets were about to be frozen. I moved a few things around but there was no way I was going to be able to disappear quickly enough. I needed someplace to go ASAP. Someplace they wouldn't be able to find me. Since they haven't been able to find you in all this time, I figured we could help each other out. The information would buy my way in. Then I found out Pollard is about to spill his guts. I'm assuming your organization has a backup plan for disappearing."

"I fear you have overestimated your worth, Agent Buchanan."

Well, hell.

"I regret that you feel that way." She stood.

There it was. The no-go she had hoped wouldn't be thrown out. Still, he had mentioned a holdout. Maybe, just maybe the game wasn't over yet.

When no one said anything else, she offered, "Since there's no place for me here, I guess I'll just have to take my chances trying to outrun the Bureau's reach. I wish you well in doing the same. They are coming, Mr. Prentiss. Trust me on that one."

A remote smile tugged at the old man's face. "Perhaps you should have done your due diligence when weighing your options, Agent. You see, once you're here, there's only one way to leave."

She didn't need a more detailed explanation.

The Council had decided her fate.

Death.

Chapter Five

"What happens now?"

As usual, the guard said nothing while he steered Sadie out of the building. She hadn't actually expected him to answer her question, but she needed to try. He was the one person who had spoken to her besides Prentiss, even if it had been only once.

And there was the man who had visited her in the dark of her cell.

Definitely wasn't the guard. His voice was different. He smelled different, too. This close it was obvious her guard wasn't freshly showered like the man who'd sneaked into her cell. The stranger who'd made that middle-of-the-night appearance had smelled clean, like soap—the kind of soap used by a man who cared how he smelled. His hair had been lighter, as well; a blond or maybe a gray.

Frankly, she hadn't encountered anyone else who met the smell-good criteria. She thought of the blond man in the room where her appearance before the powers that be had taken place. He had seemed nearer to her age. Considering his light-colored hair, he could have been the one, though she hadn't been close enough to him during the questioning to pick up on his scent.

Didn't matter, she supposed. They hadn't bought her story so living past this moment was growing more and more unlikely. Not exactly the way she had seen things going. She was still breathing so no need to give up just yet. There might be time to turn this around.

"Are you supposed to kill me?"

Her guard just kept walking, shepherding her along as he went. He wasn't so old. Early forties, maybe. It was difficult to tell. He was tall, reasonably muscled. He looked fit. The woodland greens uniform molded to strong arms and legs and a broad chest. His complexion wasn't as pale as she would have expected considering this place—wherever the hell it was—appeared to be sheltered from the sun. Now that she thought about it, the old men who'd sat around the table, the younger one, as well, had good coloring. They either had tanning beds around here someplace or these people spent time in the sun outside these walls.

But where?

Gardens? Fields? Wasn't part of the doomsday prepper thing attaining self-sufficiency? They either raised their own food or bartered with others of like mind.

"If I'm going to die, why not talk to me? It won't matter in a little while anyway, right?"

Despite her urging, he kept his mouth shut. He led her beyond the quad and all the buildings that seemed to circle the place where she'd been questioned by the group of elders or leaders. The final building they approached wasn't really a building. It was more like a massive carport. SUVs and trucks and a couple of military-type vehicles were parked beneath its expansive canopy. On the far end a long low building with half a dozen overhead doors connected to the covered parking. Vehicle maintenance, she supposed.

The guard didn't stop dragging her along until they were beyond the parked vehicles. Several small metal domes dotted the ground. At first she thought of underground gasoline tanks, but that didn't make sense since four huge tanks stood next to the maintenance building. Maybe the aboveground ones were water tanks. There had to be a water supply in here somewhere.

Her guard ushered her to the nearest dome and opened it. Beneath the metal dome was a steel wheel, the kind you would see on a submarine door. Grunting with the effort, he twisted it to the right and then raised the lid-like door upward. Beyond the door was a ladder that disappeared into the ground.

The guard straightened and reached for her secured hands. When he'd removed her restraints, he gestured to the ladder. "You go on now."

She looked from the hole in the ground to him. "What's down there?"

He stared at her a moment. "You'll see."

"Really? You couldn't think of anything more original than *you'll see*?" She ordered her heart to slow its galloping. This was that moment, the one where she had to decide if she was going to cooperate or make a run for it.

She glanced around. There was no readily visible place to run. Her guard didn't appear to be armed but that didn't mean that others who were close by weren't. Besides, where the hell would she go? And there were those guard towers.

"Running won't do you no good."

He didn't need a crystal ball or to be a mind reader to recognize what she had on her mind. "Tell me what's down there and I'll get out of your hair."

With a big put-upon breath, he said, "There are people like you down there."

"Prisoners?" She stared him directly in the eyes. He nodded.

"Are they dead or alive?" That was the big question now.

He shrugged. "Does it matter? Like I told you, there's some things worse than dying. This is one of them."

He said a mouthful with that. So much for rescuing Levi Winters. Then again, maybe he was down there, too. "Well, thanks for the heads-up."

It was now or never. If she was going to make a run for it—

"You see that hole in the wall to your right?"

His words yanked her attention back to him. "What hole?"

Even as she asked the question, a small square opened and the barrel of a rifle extended from the wall. Apparently there were guards monitoring the walls of this place from numerous vantage points, not just the obvious towers she had seen. Running would definitely be a waste of time.

"If you run, you're dead."

Made her decision considerably easier. "Got it."

Sadie put a hand on the ladder and swung one foot, then the other onto a rung. When she'd scaled down about four rungs, the squeak of metal on metal drew her attention upward as the hatch-type door closed. She drew in a big breath and let it go. Nothing to do now but see if there were any other living humans down here.

Thankfully it wasn't completely dark. Emergency-type lighting, dim though it might be, was placed along the downward path. When she reached the bottom of the ladder, a good twenty feet below the hatch, a long tunnel lay ahead of her. More of that dim recessed lighting kept the darkness at bay. The temperature was far cooler down here and there was that earthy, musty smell in the air.

Speaking of air, it was obviously pumped down

here somehow. She took another breath. Hoped like hell it was anyway.

"You're the first female we've had down here."

Sadie whipped around at the muttered words. The man stood only inches from her. How had he sneaked up on her like that? Her instincts were generally far more in tune with her surroundings.

"Who are you?" She kept her shoulders square and met his curious gaze without flinching.

Unlike the men in the compound, this man was as pale as a ghost. His hair was a stringy brown and hung down around his hunched shoulders. His clothes were like hers, sweats and a tee, only his looked old and were filthy and ragged. His feet were bare and dirty.

"George." He licked his lips. "What about you? Got a name?"

"Sadie." She braced to make a run for it but decided to hold off until she got a better indication of his intentions. It wasn't as if there was any real place to go and George here likely knew the place like the back of his hand.

"Sadie." He rolled her name around in his mouth as if he were tasting it.

She glanced around again. "What is this place?"

"The big dig." He chuckled, the sound as rusty as his teeth.

She forced her lips into a smile. "Like in Boston. I gotcha. Where are you digging to, George?"

He shrugged one of those bony shoulders. "Wherever they tell us to."

"They tell you things?" She jerked her head up toward the hatch at the top of the ladder.

"Orders. Yeah. They send 'em down along with food and water."

Thank God. That was her next concern. "So they feed you. That's good."

Another of those spasmodic shrugs. "Enough to survive. Most of the time anyway."

Well, great. Just great. "What now, George?"

"Can't say for sure. You work until we hear different." He started forward into the tunnel.

"Work?" Sadie walked alongside him. The tunnel was wide, plenty wide enough for about three people to walk side by side. Overhead, wood and steel supports kept the ground from caving in. This was no slipshod operation. Some amount of engineering know-how had gone into what they were doing.

"On the dig, of course. We're working on a tunnel headed south to Huntland. Already got one finished to Winchester."

"Sounds like a sizable operation."

He croaked another of those rusty laughs. "The Resurrection's got big plans, Sadie."

Clearly. "How many workers are down here?"

"About twenty."

"They're all prisoners?"

"Yep. Some of us were part of them before we

screwed up. I guess getting put down here was better than the alternative."

That remained debatable. "What about those who weren't part of the Resurrection?"

"Some were taken from the outside for their knowledge or skill and put down here."

"Knowledge?"

"Contractors. You know, builders. A couple ex-military guys who were assigned to the air force base."

A point she would need to pass along if she ever got out of here. "You have tools and equipment?"

"Sure." He glanced at her, his brown eyes sunken and hollow. "Lots of tools."

Sadie followed him down the length of the first tunnel and then they hit a sort of fork in the road, except there were about four different ways to go. He took the fork farthest to the left.

"Do you dig up to the surface, creating an egress or access point?" This could be a good thing.

He shook his head, deflating her hopes. "Only so far up. The rest is up to them. They do that part from above. We're not allowed to get too close to the surface."

Nevertheless, that meant those areas were closer to freedom. "Sounds like they've got it all figured out."

Her escort grunted an agreement.

The sounds of metal clanging and low voices rumbled in the distance. "We're almost to the dig where we're working now."

Ahead, the outline of bodies moving came into focus. Men wore helmets with attached lights. They swung pickaxes, hefted shovels and other digging tools. A battery-operated jackhammer rattled off. Sadie surveyed the cacophony of activity.

"This is what I'll be doing?"

George stopped and faced her. She did the same. "You give me those flip-flops you're wearing and I'll tell you."

She could do that. They were a sort of one-size-fits-all and pretty much worthless as foot protection went. "Sure."

As soon as she kicked off the footwear, he snatched the thongs and tugged them onto his grimy feet. When he'd finished, he looked directly at her and held up his end of the bargain. "We'll get the word—usually don't take long, I'd say between now and tomorrow—then we'll know whether you're a worker or supplies."

"Supplies?" A frown creased its way across her forehead. Deep inside she had a very bad feeling this was the worse-than-dying thing the guard had mentioned.

"Sometimes they stop feeding us. Like when we don't get as much done as they want. Some of us get sick and can't work as fast. They punish us then. If you're supplies, then you'll be the emergency food."

Oh hell.

He shrugged those bony shoulders again. "You'd be surprised how long even someone as skinny as you will last."

She glanced around. Said the only thing she could think to say in response to that unnerving statement. "Doesn't seem as though you have any way to keep your *supplies* from going bad."

"No need. We wouldn't eat you all at once. We always keep supplies alive as long as possible. Take an arm or a leg, then another when that one is gone. It works out pretty good. By the time the supplies is dead, we can finish off the edible parts before they start to rot."

Made an eerie kind of sense, she supposed. Unless you happen to be the main course.

No one paid much attention to them as they arrived at the worksite. The man who'd served as her guide—George—handed her a pickax and motioned to a spot for her to start. Sadie walked wide around the other workers and started hefting the ax. She couldn't help glancing over her shoulder now and then just to make sure no one was watching her. Most of the group looked like the man who now sported her flip-flops. Baggy, ragged clothes. Long, stringy hair. Filthy. Pale and weary looking.

Now that she had arrived they didn't talk so the only sounds were the pecking and scraping at the earth. The rattling jackhammer. And in those rare moments of silence, the breathing and grunting. During the next few minutes several things crossed her mind. Where did they sleep? Relieve themselves? And if she was the only female to show up, would she be raped if she tried to sleep?

Maybe she would ask George the next chance she got.

A loud sound like the single dong of a doorbell echoed through the rhythmic poking and pecking and grunting. She glanced around, her attention settling on George. He put down his shovel and started back the way they had come. The other workers looked from George to her before going back to work.

Apparently the news had arrived. Maybe dropped down from the top of that ladder the way she basically had been.

Her fingers tightened on the handle of the ax.

She supposed she would know soon enough if she was to be a permanent worker or emergency supplies.

SMITH WAITED FOR Prentiss to show up.

He'd asked for a meeting with the man immediately after the Council questioned Buchanan. The old man had decided to take his time. He knew Smith was not happy with the decision and he wanted him to wallow in his frustration.

Smith crossed the Council's private meeting room and stared out the window. For more than three decades the Resurrection had been clawing its way into this mountainside. Back then there had been only whispers about a group of doomsday survivalists sprouting up in Franklin County. No one really knew or understood what they were. Smith wasn't sure if even those early leaders of the small group understood what they would become over time.

Smith shook his head. They had become something entirely different from what they once were—from what they were supposed to be. Preparing to survive mankind's destruction of himself was one thing, preparing for a war with those not like-minded was something else altogether.

But things had escalated in the past decade. Now it was about power and greed for the few rather than the safety and survival of the many.

"Making you wait was unavoidable."

Smith turned to face the man who had entered the room. Rayford Prentiss was an old man now, but that didn't stop him from being utterly ruthless. Age had not mellowed him at all—in fact, it had done the opposite. He was as mean as hell and cared nothing for human life.

Prentiss poured himself a hefty serving of bourbon and lifted the glass to his lips. Smith watched, his patience thinning all the more with each passing moment. But he would not allow this bastard to see his mounting discontent. He couldn't let that happen until the time was right.

Soon, very soon. Sooner than Smith had anticipated.

The Buchanan woman's arrival and the name she had tossed about was a warning. Something was about to go down. Smith needed to prepare. To do that, information was required—information from Buchanan. Dropping her into the hole had been premature. The move was a blatant challenge against what Smith had suggested.

"You're displeased with my decision about the woman," Prentiss announced as he poured himself a second drink.

"She obviously has connections. Those connections could prove to be valuable."

Prentiss sat the bottle of bourbon back onto the credenza and belted out a laugh. "Because she spouted the name of a man who has been gone from here for years? If she had connections, she would know that Pollard is likely dead and buried. Of no use or threat to anyone."

"Maybe, maybe not. Either way, you're missing the big picture, old man." Smith strode toward him. "How much longer do you believe you can continue to rule these people like a dictator?"

"You believe you would be better as the head of Council."

It wasn't a question. Smith purposely made no bones about his feelings. He wanted Prentiss to know that his days were numbered. Far more so than he realized. Smith had to bite back the smile. Everything was going to change and this greedy bastard had no idea what was coming.

"You're the only one left who believes in your vision. No one on the Council agrees with your methods. They merely tolerate you out of respect for what once was."

Anger sparked in the old man's eyes. "You mean your father? I've gone too far beyond *his* vision of what the Resurrection was?"

Smith gritted his teeth for a moment. "Don't compare yourself to my father."

Prentiss moved in closer, glared up at Smith, his fury barely held in check. "You were gone for ten years. You only came back when you heard he was dead. If he hadn't named you to the Council with his dying breath, you would be in the tunnels where you belong."

The one thing that had gotten Smith through the past two years was knowing that in the end—when this was all over—he would be able to look Rayford Prentiss in the eyes and tell him the truth that no one else could know. The shock alone would likely kill the old son of a bitch.

Smith lived for that day.

Prentiss cleared his face of emotion. "You would have me change my decision about the woman."

Another statement. "You can do as you please, including change your mind."

No one questioned Prentiss. At least no one except Smith. His first month here, Smith had drawn the line in the sand. So far, Prentiss had not crossed it. He blustered and stomped all around it, but he was careful not to push too far. There were too many who remained faithful to the memory of Avery Flynn.

Prentiss wouldn't risk a rebellion. Not at this crucial juncture.

"And why would I change my mind?"

"Buchanan could prove useful," Smith said. "She didn't pull that name out of thin air. Consider how few people know what that name stands for."

Smith had him there and he knew it. Trenton Pollard had been an ATF agent. He was the only one to burrow in so deeply without being discovered. Fury roared through Smith at the memory. Pollard had burrowed deep into Resurrection. Almost took them down and then he disappeared. Except he hadn't gone far. Like the FBI agent Jack Kemp. He'd ended up buried not far from here. But Prentiss didn't know that for sure. No one except Smith knew. Although Kemp had been a casualty of the Winters family, he and Pollard had been after the same goal: the end of the Resurrection.

They weren't the first but they were the most memorable—the ones who had infiltrated the deepest.

Until now.

Prentiss made a face of dismissal. "I have my doubts as to any potential use she might prove to have."

"Are you willing to take that risk?" He wasn't. Smith was well aware that his bravado was merely for show. Particularly now that the possibility had been publicly brought to his attention. He would never give Smith that kind of ammunition to use against him if he turned out to be wrong. "At the very least she could prove a valuable bargaining chip in the future."

"Very well. For you, I will change my mind. But the risk is yours. If she becomes a liability, she will be your liability."

The two stared at each other for a long moment. Smith imagined Prentiss wished him dead. The feeling was mutual.

But not just yet.

"One day, old man, you'll learn to trust my judgment."

Prentiss made a scoffing sound. "Perhaps."

The old man walked out, leaving Smith staring after him. Rayford Prentiss would know soon enough.

Smith summoned the guard who had been assigned to Buchanan's security. He wondered if she would ever understand that she owed her life to him. If the two of them survived what was to come, he would see that she recognized what a serious error in judgment she had made coming to this place.

What the hell had she been thinking?

What had the Bureau been thinking?

He supposed it was possible this was some sort of rescue mission. Maybe for Levi Winters, though Smith didn't see him as a valuable enough target to risk the life of an agent.

Whatever had brought her here, she had put a kink in his timeline.

Now he was left with no choice but to make drastic adjustments. Otherwise everything could go wrong. The past two years of his life would be wasted.

That could not happen.

Chapter Six

Sadie did as she had been ordered and kept digging but part of her attention remained on the man coming toward her. Most of the other workers glanced her way but none dared to stop and stare. They wouldn't risk being caught slacking. The men in charge, George and three others, didn't mind bopping a slacker on the head with a shovel or nudging them in the kidneys with an ax handle. Judging by the scars on some of the workers, things could get a lot worse.

Whether it was survival or just the hint of control that came with being in charge, George and his peers appeared to take their positions very seriously. Maybe there were perks not readily visible. Obviously it wasn't clothes or a good hot bath or more to eat. Everyone in this hole looked the same as far as their state of health, ragged attire and level of filth went.

George stopped a couple of steps from her. "Come with me."

The best she could estimate she'd climbed down that ladder about two hours ago. Already blisters were forming on her hands and her muscles ached from hefting the ax. As much as she didn't look forward to days or weeks or months of this sort of hard labor, she would take that any day of the week over becoming the rest of the crew's dinner.

"Why?" Might as well know now. The whole crew would hear the news soon enough. Why keep everyone in suspense?

"They want you back up there." He jerked his head upward.

Sadie's knees almost gave way on her. "I have to go back up the ladder?"

She framed the question in a less than optimistic manner since the rest of the workers were listening. No need to rub in the idea that she was out of here. If she sounded hesitant or worried maybe they wouldn't feel so bad that they weren't the ones climbing out of this hole. Then again, there was no way to guess what waited for her up there.

There are some things worse than dying.

Still, she preferred continuing to breathe over the alternative.

"Let's go," George said rather than answer her question.

She tossed her pickax to the ground and followed the man back through the long, dimly lit tunnel. He didn't speak, just walked along, his newly attained flip-flops clacking in the silence.

When they reached the ladder, he squinted his eyes to look at her. "Somebody up there must have plans for you. Once you're down here, you don't usually go back up."

She thought of the man who had visited her in the dark and then of Prentiss. If either of them wanted her back, it couldn't be good. She would know soon enough, she supposed. If Levi Winters was still alive, he was obviously up there. She hadn't seen him down here.

"Guess so." She shrugged.

He nodded toward the ladder. "Thanks for the flip-flops."

She resisted the urge to tell him that if she had anything to do with it, he and the others would not be down here much longer. But she couldn't take the risk. Not to mention, at this point she couldn't guarantee anything. So far this mission had been an epic failure.

"Sure."

She climbed the ladder. As she reached the upper rungs the hatch-type door opened. The guard—the same one from before—waited for her. She blinked repeatedly, then squinted against the brighter light. Maybe it was coming up from the dim lighting, but she realized that the lighting was very similar to sunlight. More so than she had realized. Maybe there were solar tubes or some other discreet way of pumping in sunlight without being easily detected by anyone flying over the area.

The guard closed the hatch and glanced at her feet. He didn't ask what happened to her footwear. He probably had a good idea.

He ushered her away from the small field of domes. She decided since she'd only seen one access point while she was down there, all the other domes must be for pumping air into the tunnels.

"Where am I going now?"

He probably wouldn't tell her but it didn't hurt to ask.

As she'd expected, they continued forward without him responding. When they reached the detention center, they kept walking. Once they were beyond the Council building where she'd been questioned, they reached the area with the row of smaller buildings. He steered her toward the one marked with a number nine. At the door, he knocked and waited.

Sadie's fingers and palms burned and she wished she could wash her hands. The blisters stung. Her gaze drifted down to her feet. And they were filthy. Her pink toenails looked out of place on those feet.

The door opened and the blond man from the group who'd questioned her today stood in the threshold.

He nodded and the guard walked away. "Come inside."

This he said to Sadie. His voice was deep, curt. His silvery gaze unflinching.

Sadie did as he ordered, crossing the threshold and entering unknown territory. Nothing new. Encountering the unexpected was a major part of her mission history. If she and Levi Winters were lucky, this mission would flounder its way to success while they were both still breathing.

Her host closed the door behind her. The cabin-like structure was basically one room. A bed, table and chairs, and a small sofa were the only furnishings. On the far side of the room was a small kitchenette. A door beyond the kitchenette likely led to a bathroom. Next to the bed was a smaller table that appeared to serve as a desk since a laptop sat atop it. All the comforts of home, she mused.

He pulled out a chair from the larger, round table. "Sit."

She sat.

Rather than secure her in some manner as she'd expected, he moved to the other side of the table and sat down, his clasped hands settled on the tabletop.

"You present quite the quandary, Sadie Buchanan."

She had been told this more than once, usually by a superior at the Bureau. The words rarely turned out to be a compliment. More often, she was reminded of proper procedure and other prescribed protocols.

"Tell me what I need to do to rectify whatever the problem is." She placed her hands on the table, wanted him to see the blisters. "I'd like to know I have a place here."

He stared at her for a long while without saying more. She decided he was even closer to her age than she'd first thought. Thirty-five or thirty-six, maybe. He was tall, looked strong and his skin was unmarred by scars, unlike many of those she'd seen above and below ground in this compound. Obviously, he'd never been in a lower-level position.

"I don't trust you."

He said this in scarcely more than a whisper and still the sound startled her. He hadn't spoken in so long, she was caught completely off guard. And there was something else. The harsh whisper was somehow familiar. She studied his blond hair and then she leaned forward, putting her face closer to his, and she inhaled deeply, drawing in his scent.

It was him.

The man who had visited her in the darkness. *Smith Flynn.*

She eased back into her seat. "If it makes you feel any better, I don't trust you, either, Mr. Flynn."

He smiled. The expression was so scant she might not have noticed had she not been staring at him so intently.

"You would be wise to be grateful for my intervention on your behalf."

She met his intent stare with one of her own. "So you're the one who had me yanked back out of that hole." She hummed a note of surprise. "Interesting."

Made sense, she supposed, since she'd been brought directly here.

"Is that your way of saying thank you?"

She stared directly into those silvery eyes for a

long moment before she answered, opting to give him a taste of his own medicine. "Should I be thankful?"

He glanced at her blistered palms. "I can send you back, if you prefer. The rest of the Council recommended you for emergency supplies."

Damn. She moistened her lips, tried her best not to show how immensely grateful she was not to still be in that hole. "That won't be necessary. I am thankful you rescued me, Mr. Flynn. I suppose I'm a little worried about why you would go against all the others."

"You need a bath, Agent Buchanan."

He pushed back from the table and walked to the door. When he opened it, her guard still waited on the other side. "Get her cleaned up and put back in her cell," Flynn ordered.

"Yes, sir."

Sadie didn't wait to be told what to do next. She pushed to her feet and headed for the door. When she stood next to this man who had saved her for now, she hesitated. "Will I see you again?"

"If you do as you're told, you will see me again."

She walked out, followed the guard in his camo uniform. As usual, he said nothing. Relief sagged her shoulders. She was tired and hungry. Maybe after the bath she would be allowed to eat.

She decided to go broke on information. "I haven't seen Levi Winters. Is he in solitary or something?"

The guard didn't respond.

"He's been here longer than me," she went on, as

if he'd spoken. "Maybe he's already assigned to a job. I didn't see him at the big dig."

At the door to the detention center, he finally looked at her. "You don't need to worry about anyone but yourself. That's the way you stay alive. You do what you're told and you don't ask questions."

She nodded. "Got it."

Inside, he took her to another room, not her cell, and ordered the female in the white uniform there to see that she got cleaned up. This was only the second time she'd seen another woman. When her guard had left, Sadie turned to the other woman. "Hi."

The woman looked her up and down. "After your bath we'll do something for those blisters."

Sadie followed her to a large room that was mostly a huge shower. Three freestanding tubs sat to one side. Hooks along the wall were likely for towels. The other woman turned on the water in one of the tubs and then she left the room. More than ready for cleaning up, Sadie walked over to the tub and started to undress.

The woman returned with a towel, more of the ugly sweats and a pair of sneakers. "Size seven?" She glanced at Sadie's feet as she asked the question.

Sadie nodded. "Yes, thanks."

"Don't linger too long," the woman said. "When you're done, come back to my office."

Sadie nodded and thanked her again. The woman disappeared.

The extra-warm water felt amazing as she stepped

into it. She ignored the burn when it covered her hands. A sigh slipped from her lips as she permitted herself a moment to relax. She had earned it by God. The woman had said not to linger so she didn't. She washed her hair and smoothed what appeared to be homemade soap over her skin. When she was finished, she dried off and pulled on the clothes. Still no underwear and no socks, but she was grateful for something more than flip-flops.

She exited the shower room and walked in the direction she'd come. The only other door went into the woman's office. It looked more like an exam room. The woman got up from her desk and gestured for Sadie to sit in the only other chair.

Sadie watched as she gathered gauze, tape and some sort of salve. "You're a nurse?"

The woman glanced at her. "I am."

She was young. Midtwenties, Sadie decided. "They let you go to nursing school?"

The woman paused in her work of applying salve to Sadie's palms.

Damn, she'd obviously asked a question she shouldn't have. "Sorry. I was just curious."

"I had just finished nursing school in Tullahoma when they brought me back here."

Sadie held her gaze. "Oh."

The other woman's attention flitted away as she wrapped gauze around Sadie's right hand. "I thought I didn't want to come back but then they told me I'm getting married this year." Her face lit with a smile. "I was happy then."

Sadie moistened her dry lips. The young woman had gotten a taste of freedom during nursing school and she hadn't wanted to come back so they had dangled a carrot. "Who's the lucky guy?"

"His name is Levi. We met a long time ago but then he left. I never forgot him. I always told my father I missed him."

"Levi Winters?" Was that possible?

She nodded. "You know him?"

Sadie gave her head a slight nod rather than flat-out lie. "Who's your father?"

"Rayford Prentiss." She beamed another smile. "The head of the Council. He has many children here. Of course, we're all grown up now. My father says it's time for more children."

The picture cleared for Sadie. The Resurrection numbers were dwindling and Prentiss intended to plump up the population.

"Are there lots of married couples here?"

"Some, yes. But more are getting married this year. Some of us will be moving out, integrating into the outside communities. It's—" She snapped her mouth shut and her face paled as if she'd only just realized she had said way too much to a prisoner.

"I understand," Sadie said quickly. "It's a great plan. Mr. Prentiss is a visionary."

The other woman's smile returned. "He is. I

didn't want to see it when I was younger, but I see it clearly now."

Sadie wondered if the powers that be at the Bureau and the ATF had any idea what Prentiss was planning.

The man had his sights set on far more than this compound.

SMITH RAN HARD, pushing for another mile. There were times when he left the compound for Council business but this was the only way he left the compound on a daily basis. He ran six miles every day. Did the rest of his workout in the rec center at the compound. But when he ran he needed the freedom he couldn't get within the center running around and around a track. To find that freedom he ran through the woods. He had a route that took him through the areas where he was less likely to run into another human. Only once had he encountered another man and he'd been a hunter with no desire for small talk. He'd been on a mission that involved prey of the four-legged kind.

Smith made his usual quick stops. Leaned against a tree in one location and pretended to check his right shoe. There was nothing on the ground at the base of the tree. Nothing tucked into the moss. Then he moved on. His next stop was the sparkling stream that bubbled out from the mountainside. He knelt on one knee and cupped his hand for a drink. The water was crystal clear and cool despite the heat of the late

summer days. He scanned the rocky bottom of the
stream as he drank. Nothing. He sipped the water and
then moved on. There was one final stop, the rocky
ridge where he stopped again. This time he tied his
shoe. There was nothing tucked between the stones.

No message.

He had been certain there would be something.
A warning of some trouble headed his way. Or of
some planned rebel uprising. The one time that had
happened had secured once and for all his position
on the Council. This time, however, he'd expected
news of Sadie Buchanan's true mission. Some word
of other trouble he should anticipate. But no message had been sent.

There could be only one explanation. Buchanan's
mission was off the books, in all probability unsanc-
tioned.

She was on her own.

Damn it. He couldn't take care of a rogue federal
agent and complete his own mission. He was already
on thin ice with Prentiss.

The memory of Avery Flynn carried a great deal
of weight, as did his warning when a rebel faction
had planned a takeover. But Prentiss remained more
respected. If a choice had to be made between the
two of them, Smith would not likely come out on top.

There was one other thing he could do. He could
go down to the church and find the most recent newspaper. A message went into the classifieds only if
there was no other option. If his contact had felt he

was being watched in the woods, he would not leave a message at any of the regular drops.

Smith headed in that direction at a steady pace. His destination was just over three miles so less than half an hour was required to make the journey. He would have been able to go much faster if not for the winding, rocky paths through the woods. The paths were ones used by hunters and hikers, nothing made by anyone who belonged to the Resurrection.

He and the others were careful not to make new paths and to stay on the ones made by others. Slowing as he approached the church, Smith surveyed the area to ensure no one was about. The church was now defunct. Marcus Winters and his sister Sierra had been outed by their sister, who had recently been released from prison.

That was the way of secrets. They could only be kept for so long before they were found out.

His secret wouldn't keep much longer. He could not accommodate this unforeseen hitch. There was no leeway in his schedule for Sadie Buchanan and whatever trouble she had dragged in with her.

The church was empty as he'd expected. He walked to the road and checked the paper box that hung beneath the official mailbox. With the local newspaper in hand, he strode back to the church and sat down on the front steps. He opened the paper and carefully skimmed the classifieds. Nothing.

But the name Trenton Pollard had been a clear warning. He tossed the paper aside and stood. Some-

thing was happening and he needed to be able to prepare for whatever that something was.

What if his contact had been compromised?

There was no way to know.

Smith heaved a breath and returned to the woods.
He picked his way back to a familiar path and jogged
for a couple of miles. In the two years since going undercover he had not been faced with a situation like
this one. But he'd understood this time could come.
His contact could be compromised. The man was
older; he could very well have fallen ill or died. Time
would be required for a replacement to be situated.

The only question was whether or not Smith had
the time.

He slowed to a walk when he was within a mile
of the compound. For now there was little he could
do beyond moving forward as if Sadie Buchanan had
not suddenly appeared.

The Levi Winters issue had apparently been rec-
tified. Prentiss had decided to use him as a breeder.
Smith still found that abrupt decision strange. Had
that been the beginning of whatever was happening?
Perhaps Sadie Buchanan was not the real problem.
Maybe it was Winters.

His brother, Marcus, had been a reliable ally for
many years. Levi had been an on-again, off-again
dabbler. He had been involved with Jack Kemp—yet
another reason Smith couldn't understand Prentiss's
sudden decision to keep him for any purpose.

Smith ensured he was not being followed as he

ducked into the camouflaged pedestrian entrance to the compound. Whatever Prentiss was up to, he would keep it to himself until he was ready to move. He never shared a strategic move that involved security with any of the other Council members, much less Smith. He was far too paranoid.

There was nothing to do but remain vigilant and see how the situation played out.

Prentiss was a very astute man. He had not hung on to his position as leader of the Council by being naive or weak.

Smith supposed he should be grateful he had managed to abide the man this long. Certainly he could claim at least one record.

No one else had ever lived a lie right in front of Rayford Prentiss for this long.

Chapter Seven

"Where are we going now?"

Sadie felt grateful for the bath and the clean clothes and in particular for the salve and the bandages on her hands. But she still had a mission to attempt completing. She needed to find Levi Winters. Obviously he was still alive if Prentiss had planned his marriage to one of his daughters. Sadie decided not to try to figure out if the woman was his biological child. The idea that the old man could have dozens of children by different women made her feel ill, especially if the women had not been willing participants in the endeavors.

"The cafeteria."

Her attention slid back to the man at her side. The rumble in her stomach warned that it had been way too long since she had fueled up. No question. But maybe the trip to the cafeteria was about a new job for her. Just because she was being taken there didn't mean she would be allowed to eat.

"To work?" she asked since her guard seemed a bit more receptive to answering questions now.

"To eat."

This time her stomach growled loud enough for him to hear, too.

He grunted. She supposed that was as close to a laugh as he would permit, but she didn't miss the glint of humor in his eyes.

They entered the detention center. This time their journey took them to the left when they reached the connecting corridor that led to the cells on the right. At the end of the left corridor a set of double doors stood, the word *Cafeteria* emblazoned across the pair.

At the doors he hesitated. "Go to the serving line. Get your food and sit down. Eat and don't get into trouble. I'll be back for you in fifteen minutes."

She nodded her understanding and walked through the doors. Her guard didn't follow. There was probably a separate cafeteria for the people who belonged. There were maybe a dozen people, all wearing the same attire as she did, seated around the four tables. When she stepped up to the serving line, the man behind the counter grabbed a plastic tray and dumped beans, bread and something not readily identifiable but green in color onto the tray.

Sadie accepted the tray and walked toward the tables. Stainless steel water pitchers and cups sat on each table. The other prisoners were male. Not surprising since the number of females she had met were few and far between. The other prisoners eyed her suspiciously as she passed. She caught snatches of conversation about working in the fields or the laundry facility. There was one who sat alone at the table farthest from the serving line. He stared at his plate, visibly forcing his spoon to his mouth, chewing and then repeating.

Relief swam through Sadie. It was Levi Winters. Even in the baggy sweats and with his head bowed, she recognized him. She headed for his table, pulled out a chair and sat. Before she spoke, she reached for the pitcher and poured herself a glass of what appeared to be water. Just plain water, she hoped. Hopefully not laced with some drug to keep them under control. She still believed the man—Flynn—who had come into her room in the middle of the night had only been able to do so without her knowledge because she had been drugged with a mild sedative.

When she had downed a bite of bland-tasting beans and dry bread, she glanced at her tablemate. "You okay, Levi?"

He glanced up at the use of his name, stared at her for a moment. "Do I know you?"

She shook her head. "My name is Sadie. Your sister Cece sent me."

Hope lit in his eyes. "Is she okay?"

Sadie smiled. "She's doing great. Her name has been cleared and they've sorted the truth about what really happened when your father was murdered."

Cece had given Sadie a specific message for Levi. "Cece wanted you to know that everything is fine and none of what happened was your fault. She just wants you safe and back home."

His hopeful expression fell, and he stared at his plate once more. "They'll never let me go."

"Do you want to marry the girl?"

His head came up, his fearful gaze colliding with Sadie's. "I don't even know her. Prentiss said when I was a kid my father promised me to him for one of his daughters. He said if I didn't do exactly what was expected of me they'd put me in the tunnels." He shook his head, shuddered visibly. "I've heard about what happens to the folks who end up down there."

Nothing good. Sadie knew this firsthand. She glanced around. "Don't worry. I'll get you out of here. Just stay calm and trust me."

A frown furrowed his brow. "I don't know who you are but you're crazy if you think we'll get out of here alive. No one does. You either do what they say, or you're never seen again."

Sadie gave him a reassuring smile. "Like I said, just stay calm. Do as you're told until I tell you different."

His eyes rounded, his attention shifting over her shoulder.

Sadie glanced back just in time to see a man coming toward her. He didn't look happy. In fact, he looked angry. She stood, putting herself between Levi and the threat. "You have a problem, pal?"

The man stopped, evidently surprised that she stood up and faced him. He glared at her. "I'm going into the tunnels, because of you." He stabbed a finger into her chest. "You're damn right I have a problem."

He called her one of those truly ugly names that no woman ever wanted to be called and then he spit in her face.

Sadie swiped away the spittle with the sleeve of her sweatshirt. "I hate to hear that, but I didn't make the decision. Mr. Prentiss probably did. Why don't you take it up with him?"

His face blanched at the mention of Prentiss's name. Sadie gave herself a mental pat on the back for the quick thinking.

The man glared at her a moment longer, then walked back to his table. Sadie dragged her chair around to the end of the table and sat where she could see the rest of the people in the room. She snagged her tray and pulled it down to where she sat and forced herself to eat. Food was necessary to survival. She tasted the water—it seemed okay so she drank it down, quenching the thirst that had been dogging her since she arrived.

One by one the other prisoners in the cafeteria got up, tray in hand, and readied to leave. On their way to the tray drop, they passed Sadie, flinging whatever food they hadn't eaten at her.

She ignored them, kept shoving beans and bread into her mouth. From time to time when the food hit her in the face she flinched, but otherwise she showed no outward sign of discomfort or fear. They were all ticked off at her now. She had been pulled back from the tunnels and one of them was going in. They likely believed it was only because she was a woman. The truth of the matter was, Sadie had no idea why she'd been pulled out of the tunnels. Luck? Not likely.

"I wish I was as brave as you."

Sadie glanced at Levi. She gave him a reassuring smile. "You're doing pretty damned good, Levi. Cut yourself some slack. And don't worry, we'll be out of here before you know it."

He shook his head. "You don't understand."

Judging by his defeated expression he was more worried than relieved to know she was here. "What is it that I don't understand? I came here to find you and get you out. I will make it happen."

He swallowed hard, his throat seizing with the effort. "They're listening. I couldn't tell you. I had to do what I was told." He stood, picked up his tray. "I'm sorry. Really sorry."

As Levi walked away Sadie wondered how she had allowed her defenses and her instincts to fail her so thoroughly. She'd made an elementary mistake. One that would likely carry a heavy cost—like her life. She should have considered that Winters would have been brainwashed or indoctrinated to some degree by now.

"Well, hell."

She stood to take her tray to the drop zone but her

guard appeared. "Leave it," he said, his expression as unreadable as his tone.

Sadie deposited the tray back on the table and followed the guard out of the cafeteria. The corridor was empty. The prisoners who had thrown food at her had either returned to their cells or were back at work. The guard led her back to her cell. He held her gaze a moment before he closed and locked the door. She could swear she saw a glimmer of regret in his eyes.

If the guard was feeling sorry for her, she was definitely screwed.

SMITH STEPPED OUT of the shower and dried his body. There had to be a reason he hadn't been given additional intelligence about Sadie Buchanan via his contact. The name she had tossed out, Trenton Pollard, was a code phrase warning that trouble was headed Smith's way. But there was nothing else. No message at any of the usual drop sites.

He pulled on clean jeans and a freshly laundered shirt. The dress code was fairly simple for Council members. They wore whatever they liked. Most moved back and forth between the compound and the outside community. But not Smith. He stayed here. Didn't take chances by lingering in the community.

The guards wore the camo while the workers were issued the sweats. Only those in supervisory positions or who served on the Council were allowed to wear civilian attire. The clear distinction was one

of the things Flynn hated most about this place…
this life.

No one should be made to feel inferior to others.
One's way of life should be based on choice, not a
dictatorship led by one insane, self-centered man.
How the hell had so many been drawn into this life?
Then again, the world was changing, and those in-
terested numbers were dwindling.

A knock at his door drew his attention there. He
finished lacing his boots and stood. "Enter."

The door opened and one of Prentiss's personal
bodyguards, this one named Mitchell, stepped inside.

"Mr. Prentiss would like to see you in his private
quarters."

The old man rarely summoned Smith unless there
was a Council meeting…or trouble. Smith's gut said
this was the latter.

"Tell him I'll be there shortly."

Mitchell gave a quick nod, then left, closing the
door behind him.

Smith walked to his desk and checked the moni-
tor on his laptop. Buchanan was in her cell. Her ban-
daged hands and clean sweats told him she'd behaved
herself during her cleanup. There were no posted
complaints of trouble involving her.

She presented a conundrum. Did he tell her who
he was or did he wait for her to admit why she was
really here? Her provided story wasn't cutting it for
him. There was something more she was hiding.

Prentiss hadn't swallowed it, either. Smith's move

this morning had bought Buchanan a little more time, but he couldn't be certain how long that time would last. He had hoped to receive word from his contact this morning to give him some sense of direction. His best course of action at this point was to hold out for any intelligence that filtered in over the next few days, assuming the trouble he worried was coming didn't show first.

Taking his time, he walked to the final cabin on Council Row and knocked on the door. When his father had been alive, he had lived in cabin one. Prentiss didn't like the idea of being that available. He wanted the rest of the Council in front of him, like a wall, protecting him from any danger that forced its way into the compound.

The bastard was a coward.

"Come in."

Smith went inside. The old man sat at his table, a steaming cup of tea in front of him.

"Join me," he offered with a wave of his hand.

Smith pulled out the chair opposite him and settled into it. "I'm good, thanks," he said, declining the tea.

Prentiss sipped his tea for a half a minute before saying, "The Council has had a change of heart."

Smith remained still, his face clean of tells. "Has there been a vote I wasn't informed about?"

Of course there had been. This was how Prentiss conducted business when he wanted something his way. He didn't bother arguing his point, he simply left out the people he felt would vote against him.

"It was an emergency and you weren't available." His gaze locked with Smith's. "Apparently you were on a run or a hike. Some communing with nature."

"I do the same thing every day," Smith reminded him. "Today was no different. You're well aware of my personal schedule."

"Except something occurred while you were out," Prentiss countered. "Your new pet project, Sadie Buchanan, confessed her real reason for being here and it was not that she required sanctuary. She has infiltrated our walls under false pretenses. She represents a threat to our security."

Dread coiled inside Smith. Buchanan hadn't looked as if she'd suffered any torture for information. He couldn't see her voluntarily coming forward with this new and startling information, particularly if it cast her in a negative light.

"Really. That's an interesting development. Why don't you tell me what happened?"

"She told Levi Winters that his sister had sent her here. Buchanan was tasked with coming here to rescue him. The information she fed us was nothing more than a distraction to cover her real mission."

"I'd like to question her again," Smith said. He stood as if the recommendation had already been approved. "I'm confident I can get her full story."

Prentiss held up a hand. "No need. A final decision has already been reached. We're turning her over to the *others*. Levi Winters, as well."

Smith kept his surprise to himself. "You selected Winters for your daughter—"

"The choice was premature. He failed his final test. We don't need his kind here."

"We do need more females. Buchanan wouldn't be the first one we've swayed to our way of thinking." It was the best argument and the most logical one he could come up with at the moment.

The old man eyed him for a long while before he spoke again. "You've been her champion since she arrived. Are you suggesting you've selected her as a wife?"

Before he could answer, Prentiss went on. "You've snubbed each of my daughters, but you would have this traitor? This outlander?"

"As I said—" Smith ignored his suggestions "—she may prove useful in a future negotiation. I have not considered her as a wife, only as a bartering asset."

Prentiss announced, "The Council wants her out of our midst."

"I don't agree, and I have an equal say on Council matters." Smith held his ground. He had a vote in all matters. Prentiss understood this, no matter that he despised the idea. The bastard would not force his hand.

Prentiss stood and walked over to his desk. He picked up a document. "It is decided. The decree is signed, and the message conveyed to the *others*.

There is nothing further to discuss. You missed a great deal by being out of pocket this morning, Smith. Perhaps you should rethink your schedule in the future."

"Decrees can be overturned," Smith said, dismissing the other man's declaration. "I'll speak to the Council members."

"There will be no further discussion on the matter. You will escort Buchanan and Winters personally. Tomorrow morning."

Smith stared long and hard at him. "What are you up to, old man?"

He held Smith's gaze, then he smiled. "We make our own beds, Smith. And in the end, we have no one to blame but ourselves for the lack of comfort."

The slightest hint of uneasiness trickled through Smith's veins. This was something more than Sadie Buchanan or Levi Winters at play here.

"At sunrise in the morning you will depart," Prentiss repeated. "You should be back before dark."

Smith didn't waste any more time arguing. Instead, he left and walked straight to the detention center. The guards didn't question him as he entered, nor did anyone attempt to stop him when he walked straight to Buchanan's cell and unlocked the door.

Buchanan turned to face him. She stood on the far side of the small cell as if she'd been pacing the too-confined space. Before she could school the reaction, uncertainly flared in her dark eyes.

He went straight to the point. "What happened today?"

There were ears everywhere on this compound but questioning her was not going to change what had already been done. As a Council member he had a right to know all the facts.

"What do you mean?" She shrugged. "I was pulled back from the tunnels, given an opportunity to bathe and then taken to the cafeteria."

His irritation flared. "Do not waste my time. What happened?"

Her arms folded over her chest. "I ran into an old friend. Gave him a message from his sister. She's been worried about him."

"What exactly did you say?" Fury had him clenching his jaw to prevent saying more than he should.

She heaved a big breath as if he were the one trampling on her last nerve. "I told him who I was and that his sister had sent me to rescue him. I also told him not to worry because I would be getting him out of here."

Well, that sure as hell explained a lot. He stared directly into those dark eyes. "So you lied. Your story was a cover for your real mission."

She gave a succinct nod. "I lied."

"Get some sleep. We leave at sunrise."

He turned his back on her but before he was through the door she asked, "Where are we going?"

He didn't bother glancing back. "To trade a mole for a lost rabbit."

Chapter Eight

Sunday, August 11

They knew.

What was worse, she had told the enemy herself.

Sadie closed her eyes and shook her head. She had royally screwed up this one. Flynn had called her a mole. He was taking her from the compound today to trade her for a lost rabbit. One of the Resurrection's own, obviously, who had been taken by another group or some other faction involved with their mutual black market business dealings.

Considering she was FBI, it was possible the lost rabbit was in holding with some branch of law enforcement. The local cops? The feds? She had gotten the impression that as far as Winchester and Franklin County law enforcement were concerned—at least until the takedown at the Salvation Survivalist church—the Resurrection was more a local legend than anything else. A bunch of local yokels with guns they picked up at gun shows and MREs they ordered from the internet.

But that was not the case at all. The Resurrection was a long-term, well-planned and -operated organization with powerful contacts and an extensive reach. At this point, local law enforcement was well aware that gunrunning was involved. In Sadie's experience, drugs and human trafficking oftentimes went hand in hand with the smuggling of weapons. Maybe these daughters of Prentiss's weren't his biological children. Maybe they were stolen children he'd raised in this damned compound.

Sadie paced the few steps to the other side of her concrete cell. She had to finagle an escape. There were people in this place who needed rescuing. There was Levi and the ones in the tunnels. And possibly all the women. Though she had only seen a couple, she suspected there were more. She exhaled a big breath. This situation was far bigger and more complicated than she or anyone else had initially speculated.

It was possible another federal agency, like the ATF or the DEA, knew more than the Bureau about this group. The sharing of information was limited to a need-to-know basis for the safety of any ongoing operations and embedded agents.

She needed more information. She exhaled a resigned breath. What she really needed was backup.

The swish and whir of the lock snapped her attention to the door.

Sunrise had arrived.

The door opened and Smith Flynn met her gaze. He didn't mince words. "Let's go."

She walked toward him, expecting the broad-shouldered man to step aside so she could move through the door but he didn't. He held his ground, staring down at her.

Apparently he had more to say before this party got started.

"From this moment until I tell you otherwise you will do no thinking for yourself. You will do exactly as I say, when I say. Understood?"

Anything to get out of this prison. "Understood."

"We walk out of here, you don't look at anyone, you don't say anything. You follow me and you do exactly as I tell you."

"I can do that."

He turned and headed along the corridor. She followed. As they left the cell behind and reached the exit of the detention center, she didn't spot her guard or any others for that matter. Outside was the same. Her instincts urged her to look back over her shoulder, to look around, but she resisted the impulse. Flynn had told her not to look at anyone. She decided not to test him this early in today's game. Whatever was going to happen from this point forward, she needed to proceed with extreme caution.

She had resigned herself to the idea that she might not be able to escape this place on her own. If she couldn't get out, she couldn't get Levi out. At least if she managed to lose Flynn at some point, she had a chance of getting help back here to rescue Levi.

At this point she was more than a little surprised that Flynn hadn't restrained her hands. They headed in the direction of where she had spotted all those vehicles parked. The tunnels were in that direction, as well. Her heart instantly started to pound. She did not want to end up back down there. If that was what was about to happen, she had to do something. At least try to escape. A final ambitious effort even if she was shot for her trouble.

She bit her lips together to prevent asking him if that was his intent, simultaneously bracing for fight or flight. He'd said she was being traded. Surely that meant they were leaving the compound. Then again, the guy in the cafeteria had been fired up because he was being sent to the tunnels in her stead. That was a trade, wasn't it?

Damn it. A rush of dread roared through her veins.

She was stronger than this. If she allowed the dread and uncertainty to get to her now, she would lose all semblance of control over the situation. She might not have much as it was, but she was still hanging on to a sliver. Whatever happened, she had to cling to that modicum of control.

When they reached the motor pool, he opened the rear passenger door of a black SUV. He reached inside for something. When he drew back he had two things, nylon wrist restraints and a black hood like the one she'd worn on the way here with Prentiss and his thugs.

Movement inside the vehicle had her leaning forward just a little. Someone was already in there. The black hood concealed everything from the shoulders up, making it impossible to say if the passenger was male or female.

Flynn held out the nylon restraint and she offered her hands, wrists together, for him to do what he had to do. When her wrists were bound tightly together, he dropped the hood over her head. A hand rested against her upper arm, ushering her toward the open SUV door. She climbed in and settled into the seat.

"Where are we going?" the other prisoner asked.

Sadie recognized the voice. *Levi.* Apparently, he either hadn't received the same lecture she had or he chose to ignore the order.

The door closed and a few moments later the front driver's-side door opened, the SUV shifted slightly and then the door closed again. She resisted the urge to lift her hood and make sure it was Flynn who had climbed behind the steering wheel. He'd secured her hands in front of her so she could certainly do so but, again, she resisted the impulse. If the situation went downhill from here it wasn't going to be because she gave it a shove.

She wanted out of here far more than she wanted to satisfy her curiosity. That Levi was with her was a genuine stroke of luck. If she could salvage this rescue operation, all the better.

The vehicle started to move. About a minute later there was a brief stop, then they were moving forward again. Sadie imagined they had stopped long enough for the doors or gate or whatever to open, allowing them out of the compound. Though she couldn't see to confirm the conclusion, her heart hammered at the idea that they could very well be beyond those suffocating walls.

For the next ten minutes by Sadie's count, they drove fairly slowly. The ride was smooth, making her judgment of the speed not as reliable as it could be. Again, the urge to lift the hood and look around nudged her. She wrestled it away.

At least for now.

"Get down on the floorboard!"

The shouted order startled Sadie and for a split second she couldn't move.

"Get down!"

She tugged at Levi's arm and then scrambled onto the floorboard. Thankfully he did the same.

The shattering of glass and the pop of metal warned they were under assault.

"Stay down as low to the floor as possible," she whispered to Levi. She felt his body flatten in an attempt to do as she said.

The SUV's engine roared and the vehicle rocketed forward. The momentum of the driver's evasive maneuvers swung their weight side to side, made staying down increasingly difficult.

"Stay down," she urged the man hunkered between the seats with her.

The SUV barreled forward, swaying and bumping over the road. Sadie concentrated on keeping her body as low and small as possible. This vehicle likely wasn't bulletproof. The shattered glass she'd heard earlier all but confirmed as much. A stray bullet could end up killing one of them.

If the driver was hit…they would probably all die.

The SUV suddenly braked to a hard, rocking stop.

Another shot exploded through the rear windshield and then a detonation of new sounds. Ripping, cracking, scratching…then a hard crash.

The SUV suddenly lunged forward.

"You can get up now."

Flynn's voice, definitely his voice though it sounded muffled. Sadie recognized it was the blood pounding in her ears that smothered his words. She scrambled upward, swept the glass she felt from the seat and then righted herself there.

"We okay now?" she asked. After what they had just gone through, she figured the rules had changed. Asking if they were out of danger seemed reasonable.

"For now."

"What's happening?" Levi demanded, his voice high-pitched and clearly agitated.

"We're okay," Sadie told him, hoping he would calm down rather than grow more distressed.

She felt his arm go up. She grabbed it, hung on.

"Don't do anything until he gives the order," she reminded. "We need to get through this."

At this point, she trusted Flynn on some level whether he deserved that trust or not. But they weren't in the clear yet. She couldn't be sure of his ultimate intent. There was a strong possibility that she and Levi were only valuable if they were still alive. His risky protection measures might be self-serving.

The SUV braked to another sudden stop. Sadie's pulse sped up again.

The hood covering her head was abruptly yanked off. "Get out," Flynn ordered.

He whipped Levi's hood off next and issued the same order to him. Sadie hurried out of the SUV. Levi came out behind her rather than getting out on the other side. The road was not paved. Dirt and gravel. Muddy. It must have rained last night.

She looked up, squinted at the rays of sunlight filtering through the thick canopy of trees overhead. They were deep in the woods but they were out of that damned prison. The dirt road seemed to cut around the edge of the mountain. To their backs was the mountainside, in front of them was a steep drop-off. As she and Levi watched, Flynn stood outside the driver's-side door and guided the still-running SUV to the edge of the road. He jumped back as the engine roared and the vehicle bumped over the edge of the road, crashing through the trees.

Exactly like the one that had been firing at them,

she realized, as the familiar sounds echoed around them. That was the reason for his sudden stop back there. The other driver instinctively attempted to avoid the collision, whipped the steering wheel and ended up going over the edge of the road and down the mountainside.

Sadie watched the man walking toward them. It wasn't until that moment that she noticed the backpack hanging from one shoulder. She didn't have a clue what was in that backpack, but what she did know was that they had no transportation.

She asked, "What now?"

"Now." He pulled a knife from his pocket and sliced through the restraints on her wrists and then did the same to Levi's nylon cuffs. Flynn's gaze locked back on hers. "We run."

THE COUNCIL HAD VOTED.

Fury roared through Smith as he moved through the dense underbrush as quickly as he dared. Buchanan had no trouble keeping up with him, but Winters was slowing them down more than anticipated.

"Keep up," he shouted over his shoulder. Buchanan shot him an annoyed look.

He imagined she had some idea that they were in trouble but he doubted she fully comprehended the magnitude of the situation. The Council had decided to terminate Smith's position within their ranks and, apparently, him. They would want him and the people with him dead as quickly as possible. No loose ends. No way to trace the murders back to them.

This was Prentiss's doing. No one else on the Council would have dared to speak against Smith. The old man had grown worried that the rest of the members preferred Smith's style of progressive leadership.

He had suspected this was coming. Smith had kept his cover intact far longer than anyone expected. Funny thing was, it wasn't until Buchanan showed up that Prentiss found the perfect leverage to use toward this very end.

Smith had two choices: save Agent Sadie Buchanan's life or attempt to salvage his cover.

His cover was shot to hell.

He led them deeper into the woods. Merging into the landscape was the only way they would make it off this mountain alive. For now, they had a head start. The three-man crew Prentiss had sent after them was down. If one or more survived, it was only a matter of time before he climbed up that ravine and called for backup. Staying on the road was out of the question. There were lookouts at certain points along this stretch of road and there was no other drivable egress in the close vicinity. Disappearing between scout stations was the only option. Moving back and forth and in a zigzag pattern was their only hope of outmaneuvering the enemy.

Reinforcements would come like panthers after prey. Until then, they needed to put as much distance between them and this location as possible. Prentiss would send his team of trackers and they would bring the dogs. Time was of the essence.

Smith knew these woods. He had grown up here and he'd spent most of his time cutting paths through this dense foliage. Over the past two years he had planned for this very moment. There was never any doubt about this moment. It would come and he would need an emergency egress. He just hadn't expected to be bringing two others along with him.

There were answers he would need eventually but there was no time for that now.

"Where exactly are we headed?"

Buchanan pushed up behind him. She was strong, fit. The only good thing about the additional luggage with which he was saddled.

"You'll know when we get there."

"Those were your friends back there, right?"

Before he bothered with an answer, she fell back a few steps. "Hang in there, Levi. We have to keep going."

"Why the hell are we following him?" Winters shouted. "He's one of them."

"That's a good point."

It was the total lack of sound after Buchanan's statement that warned Smith the two had stopped.

He did the same and swung around to face the latest hurdle in this unfortunate turn of events. He visually measured Buchanan before shifting his focus to Winters. "Do you know your way out of here?"

He waved an arm to the junglelike growth around them. "We're a lot of miles from the nearest house. You'll need water. I have water. A limited supply, but I have it."

Buchanan glanced at Winters, who now stood beside her. Then she looked up, probably searching for enough of the sky to see in which direction the sun was rising.

"We're heading south," Smith advised. "And we have a long way to go. When my *friends* back there— assuming there are survivors—get a call through to Prentiss... Even without survivors, he'll be expecting a check-in. When that call doesn't come, they'll pour out in droves to find us and they'll bring the dogs. We have to move as fast and as far as possible before that happens."

"Why should we trust you?" Buchanan asked.

She was no fool. She was ready to go but she held out, no doubt to prove to Winters that she was ultimately on his side. She hoped her support would gain his cooperation. If rescuing him had been her original mission, she likely wanted to make that happen. Understandable.

Smith shrugged. "You have no reason to trust me. But I'm going. I know the way. I have the necessary supplies. You can either follow me or you can find your own way. Makes no difference to me."

He pivoted and continued his trek through the shoulder-deep underbrush.

Fifteen seconds later he heard the two coming

behind him. They were moving fast, trying to catch up. Whatever Buchanan had said to Winters, she had lit a fire under him. Good. Smith had no desire to end up dead before he'd finished his own mission.

THEY WALKED FOR another three hours before he felt comfortable allowing a water break. There was a small overhang of rocks just up ahead. They would duck under there. It would be cooler close to the earth beneath the outcropping and their position would be hidden from anyone who might be catching up to them. So far he hadn't heard the dogs but that didn't mean someone wasn't out there on the trail. Prentiss would use every method available to him. Losing more control was not an option. Smith almost wished he could see the bastard's face.

He had his doubts about the physical condition of the three who had gone over the mountainside in the other SUV. He doubted any one of them would be capable of giving chase. A call for backup would require time. Forty minutes to an hour to prepare and reach the point where the three of them had abandoned the SUV.

He scanned the trees beyond their hidden position and listened intently. By now, it was more likely than not that search parties were out there. The dogs would ensure they moved in the right direction. The head start Smith had gained was the one thing he had on his side.

Smith downed the last of his water and tucked the empty bottle back into his pack.

"Where are we going?" Buchanan asked.

"To the river. The water is low this time of year but that will work to our advantage. We'll use the water to throw the dogs off our scent."

"I haven't heard any dogs," Winters argued. "Wouldn't they be after us by now?"

"When you hear them," Smith warned, "it'll be too late." He pushed up from the rock he'd used as a seat. "Let's get moving."

He held out his hand for their water bottles. He tucked each one into his pack and headed out. Buchanan didn't hesitate. Winters did but not for long.

Rested, Smith pushed a little faster. He wanted over this ridge and to the water's edge within the hour. He wouldn't rest easy until they'd put a mile or so wading through the water behind them.

Mosquitoes swarmed when he pushed through the foliage. He ignored the occasional bite. Behind him he heard his followers swatting at the irritating insects. The ground was rockier here, making him less sure-footed. Still he pushed as fast as he dared.

By dark he would reach the safe place where he would be able to use the emergency device that would summon backup. Smith had nothing against local law enforcement in Franklin County, or the neighboring counties, for that matter, but he had an obligation to ensure there was no breach in security. The only way to do that was to use the communication device he had hidden and to call his contact and no one else.

The rumble of curt conversation droned behind him. He didn't slow down or bother to look back. He couldn't force either of them to follow him. More important, he could not share who he was or his mission with either of them, either. If they were captured, Buchanan might survive torture without talking but Winters would not.

Besides, Smith saw no reason to share that information until absolutely necessary for his own protection, as well.

"Why did my sister send you to find me?" Winters asked the woman two or three steps in front of him.

Evidently, Winters had decided to question all aspects of his good fortune. Some people just couldn't be satisfied by merely being rescued from certain death.

Buchanan kept her voice low as she answered the question. Smith didn't catch all that she told the ungrateful man. Something about his sister being worried and the local police being concerned that the Resurrection group were a more considerable threat than they had estimated.

Smith could tell them exactly how big the threat was, but he had to get out of this situation first.

"Why you?" was Winters's next question.

Smith slowed, diminishing the distance between them. He would like to hear the answer to that one.

"That's what I do," Buchanan said, practically

under her breath. "I rescue other agents or assets who get themselves into trouble."

Well, well, he'd known the lady wasn't the average federal agent. Interesting that she was a rescue and retrieval specialist.

"I guess this time isn't working out so well," Winters said with a dry laugh. "Just my luck."

"We're not beaten yet," she protested. "I've never failed before. I don't intend to start now."

Smith hoped the lady was right.

Failure would mean a very bad end for all of them.

Chapter Nine

They had been walking for most of the day. Her sneakers were still wet from the slog through a mile or more in that narrow river. The water level had been low but hopefully it was enough to throw the trackers and their dogs off their scent.

The sun was going down and the trees were thick but it was still as hot as hell. Sweat beaded on Sadie's forehead. Her legs ached. She was in damned good physical condition but this went way beyond her usual workout. This was grueling. They'd been going uphill until the past hour. The downhill journey wasn't much better, just used a different muscle group. The under-canopy brush remained thick and the landscape was rocky.

She had tried to keep Levi calm and focused on moving forward but he was resisting more and more the farther they went on the desperate journey. She wasn't sure how much longer she could keep him cooperative. His misgivings were understandable, reasonable even. But they had little choice. Keeping ahead of the enemy had to be their priority.

So far they hadn't heard any sign of the dogs Flynn had worried about. Thank God. Their stoic leader had stopped several times and listened for anyone who might be following them. He hadn't heard or spotted anyone yet. She hadn't, either, and she was keeping her eyes and ears tuned in as keenly as possible. She did not want to be captured by those bastards. Chances of surviving beyond the trip back to the compound were way less than zero.

If they were caught, they were dead.

"How far now to the destination you've targeted?" She had to admit, she was damned tired, not only physically but of blindly following orders. But she would keep going until they reached some semblance of safety or until she found reason to do otherwise.

"It's a ways yet."

Flynn said this without looking back.

Something about his nonchalance bugged the hell out of her. "Define *a ways*."

He stopped. She almost bumped into his broad back. He wheeled around, his glare arrowing in on her and she stumbled back a step.

"We've been lucky so far, let's not screw that up now. We'll get there when we get there. Just keep moving and stay quiet."

He gave her his back and started forward again.

So much for getting an update. Sadie trudged after him.

"I'm done." Levi glanced covertly at her. "I know where we are now. I just want to go home." He jerked his head toward the faint path Flynn left in his wake. "We can't be sure what he's got planned. I'd feel better taking my chances on my own from here. I can do it. You should go with me."

Sadie slowed, keeping pace with Levi. She glanced at the man disappearing deeper into the woods. "You sure about that, Levi? If they catch us, it's doubtful we would survive. Let's get through this night and we can decide how we want to move forward in the morning."

"Just let me go." He started backing away from her. "Hell, the best I can tell, he's leading us away from Winchester. My sister and the people I trust are that way." He jerked a thumb to his left.

"Let's catch up with him and confront him about your concerns." She had a bad, bad feeling about this. "We'll figure out the best option. We're safer in a group."

Levi shook his head and took off in another direction. West, Sadie decided. She went after him. As curious as she was about whatever Flynn had in mind, Levi was the one she'd come to rescue. She had a duty to keep him safe, even when he made it difficult.

She wanted to call out to Levi but she couldn't risk that the enemy was close. The last thing she wanted was to draw Prentiss's people.

She pushed harder to catch up with him. All this

time he'd dragged behind. Apparently he'd gotten his second wind. They hadn't made it far when she heard someone behind them. Adrenaline fired through her veins. She glanced over her shoulder and spotted Flynn.

Levi ran harder. Sadie did the same. But Flynn was gaining on them.

In the next moment Sadie had to decide whether to keep going with Levi or to distract Flynn, giving the younger man an opportunity to reach his sister and help. If Flynn had no real interest in what happened to them, why come after them? Why not just let them go?

Something was wrong with this scenario.

And if Levi was familiar with the area and knew the way home, why not give him a chance to make it?

Decision made, she zigzagged, heading south once more. She held her breath until Flynn shifted his direction and came after her.

She ran harder still, determined not to make it easy for him to catch her.

She sidled between two trees; her shoulder scraped hard against one. She cringed. That would leave a mark.

Keep going.

Maintaining her balance at this speed and along this rough terrain as she plowed through brush and dodged the bigger trees was not an easy task, especially downhill.

No slowing down! He was close. Only steps behind her. She could hear him breathing.

Damn, she needed to go faster.

Fingers grabbed the back of her sweatshirt. Yanked her off her feet.

They went down together, rolled in the brush. A limb poked her cheek. She grimaced.

Flynn landed on top of her, his bigger body grinding her into the brush and dirt.

"What the hell are you trying to do? Guarantee we end up dead?"

She tried to scramble away. Screaming was not an option. If there was anyone out there on their trail, they would hear.

Better the devil she knew...

"Get off me," she growled.

He glared at her for a long moment, those silver eyes icy with fury.

Then he got up, pulled her up with him and kept a death grip on her arm. He had no intention of allowing her to run again.

"That little move you pulled back there, allowing your friend—your rescue target—a chance to run, likely put a bullet in his brain or worse."

Uncertainty trickled into her chest as she struggled to catch her breath. "He knows how to get home from here. He said you're taking us in the wrong direction. Is that true?"

Frustration hardened his face. "That depends on where you think the right direction is. He's going home to Winchester? To his friends?" He laughed, shook his head. "I hope he makes it, but that's highly unlikely. They have watchers in town. Those watchers will be on the lookout for all of us. The possibility that he'll make it to help before someone nabs him right off the street is about the same as Santa paying him a visit early this year. He won't make it. Do you hear me? He. Will. Not. Make. It. Which is why we're not going directly to Winchester. I have a safe place to wait for help."

That trickle of uncertainty turned into a river. "Then I have to go after him."

When she would have headed back in the direction she'd come, he held on to her more tightly.

"You're going to draw them right to us. We have to go. We've wasted too much time already. The only way you can help Levi now is by doing exactly what I say."

She stared at him, tried to see beyond that iron mask of his. "Who are you?" She had no real reason to trust this man and yet every instinct screamed at her to do exactly that.

"You already know the answer to that question. Right now, I'm the man who's trying his best to save your life."

"How can I be sure?"

She waited for an answer, held his gaze. He needed to give her something concrete. Why would a man so high up the food chain in the Resurrection organization suddenly throw everything away and run just to save her or anyone else?

"You answer a question for me and I'll answer one for you," he countered.

"Quid pro quo," she suggested.

He gave a succinct nod.

She could do that. He pretty much already knew all there was to know about her anyway. She'd owned being a federal agent. She'd made the mistake of spilling her true mission to Levi. Beyond her last boyfriend, this guy probably knew everything there was to know about her, including her favorite college professor's name.

"All right." She braced for his question.

"Why did you use the Trenton Pollard cover story? Where did you get that name?"

"That's actually two questions," she pointed out.

He gave her a look that said he was running out of patience.

"That was the name I was told to toss out if I needed more leverage in a dicey situation."

"Who gave you the name?"

"My point of contact."

More of that frustration tightened on his face. "He or she has a name?"

She nodded. "But I'm not giving that name to you until I see where this journey ends."

He shrugged. "Fine. Let's get moving."

"Wait a minute. I get a question, too."

"So ask your question so we can go."

"Why does the Pollard name mean so much to you?"

"He's a friend of mine and I don't see how you or your point of contact could know him."

Done talking, he started forward again. She glanced over her shoulder. Hoped like hell Levi knew what he was doing. She followed Flynn. If Flynn was truly on the run, her money was on Prentiss and his people coming after him first. Finding him and Sadie was likely far higher on their priority list than finding Levi.

Hopefully that would work in his favor until he reached help.

Either way, he'd made his decision and she'd done the only thing she could: helped him escape an unknown situation.

THEY WERE CLOSE. Smith was relieved. He wasn't sure how much longer Buchanan would last. She'd held up far longer than he'd expected as it was. She was strong but they were both tired.

The safe place he'd prepared wasn't far now.

"Give me a minute."

Smith stopped, sized her up as she leaned against a tree. He shrugged off the pack and removed the last bottle of water. "We can share this one," he offered, passing the bottle to her.

This last one would have been for Winters but he'd cut out on them without any supplies. Smith wondered how far he would get before a member of Prentiss's posse caught him. Not all the way into town for sure.

He watched as she opened the bottle and downed a long swallow. When she came up for air, he said, "We're almost there."

She choked out a dry laugh. "That's what you said an hour ago. I'm beginning to think you're lost, Flynn." Her gaze locked with his. "I hope that's not the case."

"Being lost is one thing you do not have to worry about, Buchanan."

He knew this place inside and out. He'd explored every square mile in his youth. Always looking for something different, something else. He'd never found it here. Leaving had been the only way to escape this life and the people he had grown to hate. His father had been the only voice of reason among the group of preppers who had started the Resurrection. When Avery Flynn had fallen ill, Prentiss had taken over and changed things without his knowledge. He'd started to dabble in criminal activities. Smith's father had never wanted to cross that line. There had been fringes of his followers who'd gotten caught up in the black marketing of weapons and even in transporting drugs, but he'd always weeded them out in time.

But when his father lost control, it all went to hell.

Smith hadn't come back to make things right. It was too late for that. Too many of the old-timers were gone and too much of the younger blood was greedy and power hungry. The extremists without conscience had taken over. He'd come back to take them down. It wasn't what his father would have wanted but his father had been wrong. Anywhere those with extreme attitudes and beliefs gathered, nothing good came of it.

Ever.

"Fifteen minutes," he assured her. "We'll reach our destination in fifteen minutes—barring any unforeseen events."

She screwed the cap onto the water bottle and tossed it to him. "I'm holding you to that."

He downed a long swallow and put the remaining water away. Before he could stop himself, he licked his lips and savored the taste of her. Sadie was different from any woman he'd ever met. She was stronger, determined, loyal. Intelligent. Unconditionally fearless. She stirred his interest in numerous ways.

Shaking off the distraction, he started moving forward again. "Let's go. We don't want to fall behind schedule since you're holding me to it."

She laughed again. He liked the sound of it. "You're a smart guy, Flynn."

Maybe. He hadn't considered himself smart in a long time. The truth was, he hadn't even considered the future until very recently. He had resigned himself to the idea that he would likely die getting this done.

Still could. It wasn't over yet.

The underbrush was thinner here in the rockier soil. Made going a little easier. Being physically exhausted, however, made just moving a chore. It had been a long day. Buchanan wasn't the only one who was beat.

They made the fifteen-minute timeline with a couple of minutes to spare. He pointed to a copse of trees that hugged the mountainside maybe ten yards below their position. The relief on Buchanan's face was palpable.

The overgrowth was thick around the cave opening. He carefully pushed the limbs aside and ducked inside first. There were times when a man should go first—like when he needed to ensure there were no wild animals, no den of snakes holed up in his safe place. Buchanan would likely argue the point with him but there were some things his father had taught him that stuck. *Always protect those under your care.*

Something else she would argue. Fiercely, no doubt.

He tugged the flashlight from its holder on the side of his pack and scanned the small shelter. Clear. No sign of animals. As often as he could get out here he sprayed the area with repellant to ward off animals but some critters weren't so easily put off. Thankfully the place was clean, no animal droppings. No snakes.

"You can come in." He held back the limbs, ensuring he didn't break any. Those limbs acted like a curtain, providing a layer of camouflage.

Once she was inside, he used his flashlight to locate his stored supplies. The cave was only about fifteen feet deep and the last five or six feet narrowed down to the point where crawling was the only option. He'd banged his head plenty of times. At the very back, he carefully moved the stacked stones he'd gathered in the immediate area. All looked exactly as if they'd always been right here in this pile. He'd gone to a great deal of trouble to ensure no one who might stumble upon this place noticed his stored goods.

Beneath the stack was a nylon bag, pale gray in color, nearly as large as his pack. It was sealed in a clear plastic over bag. Inside he kept his emergency supplies. The plastic was to better protect them from the elements and to ensure the bears and wolves didn't pick up on any scents.

His gut growled as he set the ready-to-eat packets aside. They'd only had a couple of protein bars today. It was time for something a little more substantial.

"What's all this?" Buchanan moved in next to him, sat back on her knees.

"Dinner. A burner phone. Weapon. First-aid supplies." Not so much of the latter but enough to get by in a minor emergency. A packet of blood-clotting agent, a suture kit. Antibiotic salve and a few bandages. "Water. A small blanket. Emergency light. You know, the usual."

There was also a backup plan, which he pocketed without mentioning. He tucked the nine millimeter into his waistband and loaded most of the other supplies into his pack. "You want beef or chicken?"

She studied the two packs of ready-to-eat meals. "I'll take the chicken."

"Good choice." He passed it to her and grabbed the beef.

He moved back to the roomier portion of the cave and opened up the small emergency light. He sat it on the ground. The lumens were low but he didn't want it glowing beyond the cave opening. It was enough. He tossed his guest the thin blanket. It wasn't much but it was better than nothing when one was sleeping on the ground.

"You can use that tonight. I'll use my pack for a pillow. I don't mind sleeping on the ground."

"So we're staying the night here?"

He shrugged. "If that's what it takes."

While she opened the food pack and ate, he fired up the burner phone. Once it was on, he moved to the cave opening to get better service. With a few taps, he sent the necessary message. The phone's battery was way too low. He'd charged it the last time he was here. With it turned off it should have maintained the charge. When the message had been delivered, he relaxed. He returned to where Buchanan sat and settled in for however long they had to wait.

He opened his meal pack and ate slowly, more slowly than he wanted to but it would satisfy him better that way. Buchanan did the same. She'd likely had similar training and understood the need to adapt to extreme change. Being a field agent required a degree of flexibility. That she consumed every bite of the less-than-tasty meal confirmed his conclusion.

When she'd finished, she said, "Tell me about the message and why we may be here all night."

"The message goes into a pipeline of sorts. It takes a while to get to the intended recipient. Once he has it, he'll make arrangements for a pickup. When the pickup is ready, we'll go to the designated location. There are several good options within two miles of our position."

She sipped on the packet of water. "The contact is aware of this location?"

He shook his head. "No one knows this location. It's a security precaution in case there's ever a breach in our communications. I selected this location based on my knowledge of the area and the best egress routes. We agreed upon designated pickup points. The gap allows for a degree of separation between me and any trouble that might crop up. As I'm sure you're well aware, advance preparation is key."

She nodded but then frowned. "What if you're injured? You might not be able to make it to the pickup point."

"That's where my backup plan comes into play." He patted his pocket. "I have a beacon, the same technology skiers use. If necessary, I turn it on and they can find me."

Her expression told him she was impressed. "You've got all the bases covered."

He focused on his food for a while, let the silence fill the space. It would be dark soon. Since there was no way to know what time they would have to move, it would be best to get some sleep now while they had the opportunity.

When he'd finished his meal, he put the packaging into his pack. "Sleep if you can. We may have to move again at any time."

He checked the screen on the burner phone before sliding it into his shirt pocket. With the phone on vibrate and the pack as a pillow, he stretched out for a quick nap, braced his arms over his face. He hoped like hell the charge lasted until he had a response.

He listened as Buchanan spread the thin blanket out on the ground and did the same. She lay there quietly for about a half a minute. He was surprised she lasted that long.

"What are you, Flynn? If you tell me you're just a run-of-the-mill member of that group we escaped, I'm going to know you're lying."

At this point he didn't see any reason to keep her in the dark. "I'm like you."

She rolled onto her stomach. He felt more than saw the move. "Only way different."

He chuckled and lowered his arms. "Not so different."

"Come on. You don't work for the Bureau or I would know. The ATF didn't claim you. Neither did the DEA. Since when does Homeland Security embed agents in the middle of nowhere like this?"

This time he outright laughed. "I'm not with Homeland Security. I'm with the ATF."

She lay there for a moment seeming to mull over what she'd learned. It wouldn't be unusual for an embedded agent to be denied for the purposes of protecting the mission. Like the military, need to know was the motto for most federal agencies.

Finally she asked, "How did that happen? Did someone recruit you?"

"No. I recruited myself."

She waited for him to go on but he didn't. He should have realized she would want his story as soon as she knew the truth about who he really was, but he wasn't sure he wanted to share it. It felt too intimate.

Or maybe he was afraid it would turn the *moment* into something intimate. It was essential that they stayed focused. Emotions could not get tangled up in this precarious situation.

"I'm waiting for the rest of the story, Flynn. Don't leave me hanging like this."

"I grew up in Franklin County. My father was one of them, only not like what you see today. It didn't start out that way. But I watched it happen and I hated it, hated the men who made it happen. I made my way into the ATF for the sole purpose of coming back here and taking Resurrection down. For years I pretended that wasn't my motive. I tried to be a good agent, take the assignments given. Do the job to the best of my ability—whatever that job might be. But I couldn't forget. Two years ago when my father died, I approached the top brass with an offer. They accepted and I came back to do what needed to be done."

"Wow. That's a hell of a story, Flynn. You must have incredible restraint. You've had to pretend to be one of them for two whole years."

He rolled over her comment for a time and then he said, "I've always been one of them. I'm just not like them. That's the difference."

She nodded. "I get it."

"What about you, Agent Buchanan? How did you become a rescue and retrieval specialist?"

"Growing up in Montana I always said I wanted to work where the sun shines all the time and there's no snow so I ended up in Miami. I was so new it was painful but because of my obvious Hispanic heritage, I was needed for a particularly high-profile assignment right off the bat. They wanted me to get inside and evaluate the situation with a deep-cover agent who had gone silent. Getting in was easy. I have a knack for putting people at ease and making them believe what I want them to believe."

"You do." If it hadn't been for her using the Trenton Pollard name, he could have fallen for her story. She was good.

"Not only did I find the guy but I got him out using my favorite bait-and-switch tactic. It almost never fails."

"Is that right?"

"That's right. I make the bad guy believe he's going to get one thing and then I do exactly the opposite of what he expects."

He chuckled, couldn't help himself. This was a woman who enjoyed her work.

"Turns out my target was the grandson of a former director. He was so impressed with my work, he urged the powers that be to make better use of my skill set. So here I am. This was basically a favor. An off-the-record mission."

"Well, Agent Buchanan, it's a pleasure to make your acquaintance." He thrust his hand at her.

She grinned and gave it a shake. "Ditto, Agent Flynn."

Now if they could only get themselves out of this thorny situation, maybe he'd ask her out to dinner.

A frown furrowed his brow. The beef jerky obviously hadn't done its job or he wouldn't still be thinking about food.

Then again, maybe it wasn't food on his mind.

He peeked at the lady lying so close.

Too dangerous, he reminded himself.

Maybe another time when they weren't both targeted for execution.

Chapter Ten

Monday, August 12

The way Flynn kept checking the burner phone, Sadie was reasonably confident he was worried more than he wanted her to know that there had been no response from his contact and the phone's battery was dying.

He hadn't said as much but she was no fool. There was no way a crucial reaction to a critical situation would take this long. She pulled her fingers through her hair, wished she had a brush. She shifted her position a bit—this rock was not made for comfort. Being stuck in this cave all night was even less so. She was thankful for the protection from the elements and the enemy but even when she slept, fitfully to say the least, she was aware of *him* next to her. The smell of his skin, the heat emanating from his body. Not helpful when trying to sleep. At least not when she wanted desperately to do something entirely unrelated to sleeping.

Not smart, Sadie.

The situation wasn't completely unexpected. She had been so focused on her career for years now that she'd totally ignored her personal life. Sure, she had the occasional date with some guy a friend insisted she so needed to meet. Very rarely did that develop into physical gratification. Apparently, that was an issue. She was like a starving animal now, desperate...

She rubbed her hands over her face and wished for a long, hot bath. Maybe a trip to the spa the way she'd done years ago—before her career took over her life. There, she decided, was the real source of the rub. All her female friends—the ones with whom she'd done lunch and spa days—were married. Most had children. They all thought because Sadie was approaching thirty-five that she should be doing the same. It wasn't really because they were old-fashioned or had narrow views, it was just human nature. The heightening urge to procreate as one reached thirty.

Sadie had passed thirty several years ago and not once had she thought about a permanent relationship, much less kids.

She worked. Work was her constant companion, her best friend, her lover.

Her traitorous eyes stole a glance at the man packing up their sparse campsite. But this man had her dwelling on her most basic instincts. Of all the times for an attraction to form, this was the absolute worst possible one.

The guy was a stranger—no matter that she now knew he wasn't a criminal—and their situation was dire at best.

Before daylight he'd gone outside their hiding place and checked the area. When he'd returned, she had taken a turn slipping out of the cave to go for a necessary break, as well. Flynn was good at concealing his concern but she hadn't missed his mounting tension. It was in the set of his broad shoulders, the lines across his handsome forehead.

He was worried.

Which made her worry.

It was possible, she supposed, that there had been a delay due to some unpredicted issue. But they had gone well beyond that possibility now. This was not just a delay, this was a total breakdown in the link between a deep undercover agent and his primary support contact.

When Flynn pulled on the pack, she asked the question burning in her brain. "What's the plan now?"

"No response from my contact. The phone's battery is dead. We move on. Staying here any longer would be a mistake. As well hidden as we are, the dogs could pick up our scent again."

"Agreed." For the first time this morning she thought of Levi. She hoped he had made it to someplace where he could call someone he trusted. Things would have been a lot simpler if he'd stayed with them. She glanced at the man towering over her. A lot simpler on numerous levels.

"Stay close," he reminded her, "and move as quietly and quickly as possible. We'll head off this mountain and into town via trails that keep us out of sight and away from where we would most likely run into people."

Which meant they would be hiking a lot of miles, taking the longer, tougher routes. The blisters forming on her feet ached. They weren't as bad as the ones on her hands, but they were getting there. She glanced at the bandages, considered discarding them but decided against it for now.

At the opening that would take them out of the shallow cave, he hesitated. "We'll save the backup plan for later. I have no way of knowing what's gone wrong with my communication link so I don't want to give anyone our location until we know whether the one who receives the signal is friend or foe."

So, she'd been right.

He parted the thick foliage and made his exit. Sadie followed.

Whatever happened now, they were on their own.

Smith had no choice at this point but to admit that his contact was either dead or he'd turned.

He had known the man who was his primary backup for a decade. He found it difficult to believe he could be turned. Odds were, he was dead. The mistake was Smith's. He had insisted on only one person having knowledge of his egress options. He should have known better than to rely on only one man. Humans were not immortal. Accidents happened, health issues cropped up. One or both stealing lives at inopportune moments. Things happened, infusing desperation, weakening even the strongest man.

Choices at this juncture were extremely limited but at least they still had a couple.

Smith had decided that they would keep moving. Yesterday had been spent traveling in wide circles up and then down the mountain. No express routes. Today would be somewhat more direct. He would use a scatter pattern to prevent leaving a straightforward trail to follow. However hard he tried not to leave signs of their presence, it was impossible not to break the occasional small branch or trample plants.

Their path wouldn't be difficult for a trained tracker to follow. The dogs wouldn't need anything but their scent.

Frankly, Smith was surprised he hadn't heard the dogs at some point yesterday. Particularly after Winters separated from them.

This, too, was cause for concern.

Was Prentiss so certain he would win that he didn't bother sending a search party?

The idea hadn't crossed Smith's mind until his contact failed to come through and time had continued to lapse without trouble finding them.

Now that he considered the possibility, Prentiss

had been the one to insist Smith take Buchanan and Winters to the *others*. If he'd discovered Smith's secret, why not kill him at the compound? Was the old bastard's intent to make an example out of him? Show his followers who their true protector was?

This was more wrong than he had realized.

There was a mole all right, but it wasn't Buchanan. It was someone on Smith's home team. Someone in the ATF with clearance to this mission. Only a handful of people knew about this cleanup and infiltration detail. Still, that didn't mean someone with the opportunity hadn't found a way to access the files. The world was one big electronic filing cabinet these days. Nothing was unattainable if one knew in which drawer to look and possessed the skill to open it.

Had Prentiss turned someone with that kind of know-how?

The only way to be sure was to get Buchanan to safety and then for him to return to the compound for Prentiss. This was a finale that required an up close encounter.

He had spent the past two years of his life digging deeply into the Resurrection. He was not going to walk away without eliminating the organization, even if that meant taking matters into his own hands.

The compound had been built into the mountainside. It was completely camouflaged and protected by the earth itself. Over and over he had mentally plotted where and how the explosives would need to be planted to destroy the place—to bring down the entire mountainside. The problem was, as gratifying as that result would be, it wouldn't change anything. Some of the powers that be lived outside the compound. They hid themselves among the locals to stay aware of whatever was going on in the rest of the world. Having everyone with power, reach and contacts in the same place at the same time for elimination would be virtually impossible.

Smith had toyed with that scenario a thousand times.

Once the compound was destroyed, those who survived would go into hiding. He knew them all— every single one. But sending them to prison for their criminal activities required solid evidence, none of which he possessed outside that compound. Even lining them up for vigilante-style termination would require an army. The moment one was taken out, the rest would scatter like crows. Since he didn't have an army prepared to commit cold-blooded murder, he needed a better plan.

A laugh tugged at his gut. In two years he hadn't been able to come up with a workable strategy.

He could sever the head of the snake, Prentiss, but another one would sprout in his place.

Unless…he found a more lethal snake willing to swallow up the competition entirely.

A new plan started to form. Smith had a feeling this one might even work. But to make that happen he would need to enter the territory of that lethal snake.

It was a good plan. He thought of the woman right behind him. Rather than attempt to explain the intricate details and to persuade Sadie to go along, he decided to keep her in the dark. She would be mad as hell when she found out, but if he accomplished his ultimate goal, she would forgive him.

He hoped.

Altering his course, he headed for dangerous territory. He readied for trouble, exiling all distraction in order to focus fully on his surroundings, listening and watching. Within the hour they would cross into territory ruled by another group. They couldn't really be called an organization since they weren't technically organized. These people didn't even have a name, much less a motto. Anyone who knew them merely called them the *others*. The one thing Smith knew for certain about them was that they were dangerous. Cunning and methodical.

Maybe clinically insane. Certainly crazy by anyone's measure.

Crazy was what he needed at the moment.

All he had to do was find it without getting Buchanan or himself killed.

THEY WERE TRAVELING in a different direction now. Yesterday he had done the same. Flynn had wound back and forth around this mountain. She'd figured his goal was to make their path more difficult to find and follow. With no response from his contact and no sign of Prentiss's people or dogs, she had expected he would take a more direct route today.

Maybe not.

She wanted to ask him about his plan, but he'd reiterated that silence was particularly important today. Rather than risk making too much noise, she'd kept her questions to herself for now and followed his lead. If she had to find the way out of here they would likely end up bear bait in these damned woods.

Not that she'd spotted any bears or bear tracks but there could be bears, coyotes or wolves, to name a few predators who would present a problem.

There was the gun he'd had hidden in the cave. But she didn't have any idea how much ammunition Flynn had on him. Maybe only what was in the weapon. Maybe not enough to survive if they were attacked by man or beast.

But they had their wits, no shortage of determination and Flynn's extensive knowledge of the area.

The situation could be a lot worse.

A muzzle jammed into the back of her skull. Before her brain had time to analyze how it happened so fast without her noticing someone was closing in on her, her body instinctively froze.

"Don't move."

Somehow she had known the person—man obviously—on the other end of that barrel was going to say those two words.

Smith spun around, his weapon leveled on the threat. "Back off," he warned.

Before his growled words stopped reverberating in the air, three more men stepped forward, rifles aimed at him.

Sadie blinked, startled when she'd thought nothing else could shock her. The men wore paint, like body paint—nothing else as far as she could tell. They had melted into the landscape and only when they moved had their presence become visible. She blinked again to ensure she wasn't seeing things.

"Back off," Flynn repeated. "Aikman is expecting me."

If these were more of his friends, it would have been nice if he'd given her a heads-up before the one behind her startled the hell out of her.

One of the three fanned out around Flynn stepped forward, moving closer to him. "Drop the gun."

Sadie held her breath. Agents were trained never to relinquish their weapons but sometimes there simply was no other choice. An agent learned through experience when it was time to forget the classroom training and do what had to be done.

Flynn tossed the weapon to the ground and raised his hands. "My name is Smith Flynn. Take me to Aikman."

The guy behind Sadie shoved a bag at her. "Put this on."

Sadie took the bag and tugged it onto her head. The last thing she saw before the black fabric fell over her eyes was Flynn with the business end of a rifle stuck to his forehead.

The nearest muzzle nudged her back. "Start walking."

She did as she was told, hoping like hell she didn't trip over a tree root or a rock. No one talked but she heard the faint sounds of their new friends moving through the underbrush. She suddenly wondered if the painted guys wore shoes or boots or something on their feet. She hadn't noticed. The guy behind her was probably painted, too. He was, she decided as she recalled the arm that had thrust the bag at her.

The only good thing was that Flynn appeared to know who these people were. This Aikman, she assumed, was someone in charge. Hopefully someone high enough up the food chain to keep them from becoming "emergency supplies."

Her toe snagged on a root or a rock and she almost face-planted. Thankfully, she managed to grab back her balance. Her sudden stop to capture her equilibrium won her another nudge from the muzzle.

Sadie counted off the seconds and minutes. By her estimate, they walked for half an hour. The terrain didn't change much. Brush, rocks, moving sometimes up, sometimes down. The scent of food cooking told her they had reached a camp of some sort. She doubted it was noon yet but it was past midmorning. No matter that she'd had a protein bar very early that morning, her stomach sent her a warning that she needed to eat again soon.

And coffee. What she would give for a big, steaming cup of coffee.

She wondered if this group would have a compound built into the mountainside like the Resurrection. She had to admit, the idea had been ingenious. A hand suddenly rested on her left shoulder. She stopped, braced to either fight or run like hell. The bag whipped up and off her head.

She blinked twice, three times, and surveyed the area. There was a canopy of green overhead. A combination of trees and vines and other plant life she couldn't readily identify. Sunlight filtered through, making her blink with its brightness after wearing the bag. There were shacks made of branches, twigs and brush. This didn't look anything like a compound. These were like primitive huts that flowed seamlessly with the brush and trees. She looked upward again, spotted similar builds in the trees. The tree houses were also constructed with limbs and other pieces of the surrounding natural resources, making them almost like an extension of the trees.

Another nudge in the back and she started walking again. Flynn walked ahead of her, a painted man on either side of him. They moved deeper into the trees. Finally they reached an area that looked very much like the place against the mountainside where they'd slept last night. Brush and branches hid a narrow cave opening. They were escorted inside where two more men, these wearing dark clothes similar to SWAT gear, took over escort duty. The man who'd been behind Sadie all that time and his friends slipped back out the way they had come.

Beyond the opening, the cave widened into a room. There were lights in the cave but not electric lights. The lanterns looked like the old oil type. The cave floor was rocky. Water trickled from the walls here and there. Smelled musty. No more food smells. Whoever had been cooking, they were outside in the rustic camp they'd passed through.

This cave was far larger than the one they'd called home last night. The ceiling zoomed several feet overhead and the width of the space was five or so yards. They moved downward from there. Maybe a more elaborate compound had been built deeper in the cave.

The wide tunnel divided and they took the left fork. A few yards in they passed another wide room-size section on the left. Rows of rustic tables filled that space. Dozens of oil lamps lit the area. People dressed in white coveralls like painters and wearing paper face masks were frantically packing some sort of product.

Oh hell.

Drugs.

Her stomach sank. This was one of those things you couldn't unsee. People in this business didn't allow outsiders to see their work and walk away.

This was bad.

She hoped like hell Flynn knew what he was

doing. She also hoped he knew these people really well—well enough to share dark secrets.

Otherwise they were goners.

Once they had moved beyond the workers in the white suits, they passed a number of large round stones that sat on either side of the corridor. The lead man stopped. With obvious effort he pushed one of the stones aside, revealing a hole in the rock wall, like a large round doggie door without the flap.

Not exactly a user-friendly entrance to wherever they were going next.

"Inside." The man looked at Sadie as he said this.

She glanced from him to the hole. Was he serious? She shifted her gaze to Flynn. "I'm supposed to go in there?"

"For now. Don't worry."

He couldn't be serious.

The man with the gun waved it as if he was running out of patience.

Great. She squatted, then dropped onto her hands and knees. She poked her head far enough through the opening to see what was inside. Nothing. As best she could determine it was just an empty, small, cube-like rock room. She crawled inside. Squinted to get a better look at the space. She shifted, scanning all the way around while there was still light filtering in from the open hole. In the corner to the left of the hole she'd just entered her gaze snagged on a form. She crawled closer, her eyes adjusting to the even dimmer light.

Bones.

Not just bones. An intact skeleton.

The rotting clothing suggested the owner of the bones had been male.

She swallowed back a sound, not exactly a scream but something on that order.

The noise from the stone rolling in front of the hole once more rumbled around her. She sat down on her bottom and stared at the only exit from this new prison. A dim outline of light from the lanterns in the corridor slipped in past the stone now blocking that exit.

Her gaze shifted back to the bones. She couldn't really see them now but her brain filled in the details from the picture seared into her memory.

Whoever had been stuck in here before had died in this place.

Without water or food it wouldn't take that long.

She thought of the lack of tissue on the bones. The person had been trapped in this place for a very long time. Years. Maybe as much as a decade considering the deteriorated state of the clothing he wore.

Sadie sat in the middle of that musty, dark space and replayed the past decade of her life. She had graduated with a master's degree and some big plans. Two summer internships with the Bureau and she was accepted as soon as she reached the age requirement. Her parents had been so proud. Her mother had been a little concerned about her daughter going into law enforcement, but she'd come to terms with the decision after the first year. Maybe it had been Sadie's excitement that had won over her mom.

Sadie had ended the relationship with her hometown boyfriend before entering training. The long-distance relationship had basically been over since undergrad school anyway. They were going in different directions with changing objectives. Why prolong the misery by watching the relationship they had once believed would go on forever shrivel up and die? Strange, she never once considered when the relationship ended that it would be her last one.

Dates, never more than three, maybe four with the same guy. Her social calendar consisted more of bridal showers, weddings and baby showers for friends than dates for herself.

If she died in this dark, dank place her parents would be devastated.

A life half lived.

Not true, she decided. If she died in this place, she would be dying young, for certain. But it wasn't a life half lived. She had lived every single day to its fullest. She had loved the hell out of her work. She had helped to bring down numerous bad guys and she had rescued more than her share of good guys.

"Get over it, Sadie. You are not going to die in this hole in the ground."

She pulled up a knee and rested her chin there. She would find a way out of here. It was what she did. And she was really, really good at it…usually.

As soon as Flynn finished his meeting with this

Aikman person and was brought here, they would put their heads together and come up with an escape plan.

Flynn had a contact with these people. He hadn't appeared worried when they were captured. She shouldn't be worried, either. Then again, Flynn's record with his contacts hadn't actually been a reassuring experience so far.

Maybe it was time to get worried.

Chapter Eleven

Smith had waited a half hour. The cuckoo clock on the wall counted off every second with a loud tick-tock. Any minute now the bird would slide past its door and count off the hour: 11:00 a.m.

He forced himself to relax. He possessed as good an understanding of these people as anyone. They did things their way in their time. Making him wait was a way of showing dominance. As long as he was still breathing there was reason to believe an arrangement could be reached.

This move had been a risk. A risk he was wagering everything would work out. Unfortunately, the wager involved Buchanan's life as well as his own. If things didn't work out as he intended, her death would be on him. That was the one part that didn't sit well with him. But they were in a no-win situation. As a trained agent, she would understand the need to take drastic measures.

Smith drew in a deep breath and reminded himself to be patient. To play the game.

The tunnel where Buchanan had been secured had forked again, leading to the outside once more. Another campsite had been built against that side of the mountain. Again, using elements that blended in with the environment to keep them off the radar of reconnaissance flyovers.

Aikman's office was like any other with a desk, chairs and electricity. The electricity was furnished by a generator. The primary difference between this place and that of the Resurrection as far as Smith could see was the absence of electronics. The *others* didn't use electronics with the exception of burner phones, which they used sparingly. They stayed as far off the grid as possible.

The door behind Smith opened and Aikman entered, minus his usual bodyguards. They no doubt waited outside the door. No matter that he was well aware that Smith was unarmed, he would never take the risk of being alone in a room with a known follower of the Resurrection without backup close by.

"You got some nerve coming here after what you did, Flynn." Aikman sat down behind his desk. "I was expecting you to deliver two packages yesterday. Prentiss and I had a deal. First, you don't show, then I get word you've dropped off the grid. Now you waltz in here with only one package." He shook his head. "This is not good."

Draven Aikman was younger than Smith. His rusty-brown hair was kept skinhead short but his beard was long, at least ten or twelve inches. He wore the same dark uniform as his soldiers. He'd killed the old man who held the position as leader before him. The story was that the old man was sick, practically on his deathbed and making bad decisions. Aikman claimed he took care of the failing part for the good of the whole. Whatever his motive, he now held the highest position among this closed, clannish group known only as the *others* by the few who were aware of their existence.

Aikman propped his feet on the desk and leaned back in the chair, eliciting a squeak of protest from the base. The desk and chair, like the rest of the furnishings, might have been unwanted castoffs picked up from the side of the road on garbage day. The *others* had a reputation for living free of excessive material burdens. Survival of the coming human self-annihilation was their singular goal. Still, they were only human and not completely immune to power and greed. In any group there was always someone who couldn't resist the temptation of *more*.

"You suddenly develop a death wish?" Aikman asked. "Coming here, throwing my name around like we're friends. I could get the wrong idea."

"The deal Prentiss made is off. I'm here with a different offer."

Aikman lifted his brows. "This better be good."

"There are other names on my list," Smith warned, "but I chose to bring this offer to you first."

The other man's gaze narrowed. "What kind of offer?"

"We both know the Resurrection is your primary competition. We've blocked your every attempt to expand your operation into other areas. You've been stuck making the drugs no one else wants to make unless they have no other choice. We've pushed you out of the arms business. Basically, we've kept you down for decades."

"If you're supposed to be buttering me up for some proposition," he laughed, a rusty sound, "you're falling way short of the mark."

This was the mistake most people made. To look at the *others* and how they lived, one would automatically think uneducated, backwoods hillbillies. But that was not the case at all with the ones like Aikman. According to Smith's sources, the man had a master's degree in business administration. He was smart. Allowing you to believe he wasn't automatically put you at a disadvantage in any negotiation.

"I'm sure you get my meaning," Smith said, ignoring his dig. "I've decided it would be in both our best interests to join forces. We both have our resources. If we pool those resources, we could expand our operations and take over the Southeast."

Aikman dropped his feet to the floor. "You want me to believe that you're ready to abandon your loyalties to the Resurrection—an organization that runs in your blood? You would trample on your daddy's memory?" He grunted a sound of disbelief. "Pardon me if I don't believe you. What're you up to, Flynn?"

This was the risky part. It would have been easier for Smith to keep walking. To climb down this damned mountain and turn himself over to local law enforcement. He would have been sent back to where he belonged ASAP. The mission would have been over and the goal he'd dedicated his entire existence to for the past two years would have been lost forever.

He would have been alive, safe and free of this nightmare.

Except Prentiss would have gotten away. He and his Council of ruthless killers would have relocated and continued doing whatever they pleased with no care of the human cost. No worry about what the guns and the drugs were doing to society.

Smith was left with one option—finish this in the only way possible: light the fuse of the Resurrection's number one enemy.

Start a war.

"Prentiss sold me out," Smith confessed. That part was true. Rumor of the shake-up would get around soon enough if it hadn't already.

There was no other explanation for the trio who'd showed up behind them on that mountain road after they left the compound. Prentiss had intended to wash his hands of Winters, Buchanan and Smith.

End of story. To believe they had appeared for any other reason would be foolish. Somehow Prentiss knew. Which would also explain the sudden drop in communications with Smith's contact.

Whatever had gone wrong, Smith was on his own. He had few options if he wanted to finish his mission and this was the best one.

Aikman reared his head back and considered the announcement for a moment as if he didn't quite believe what he'd heard. He pursed his lips then rocked forward, propping his forearms on his desktop. "You actually expect me to believe that Prentiss dared to attempt a coup so he could be rid of you?"

"Believe what you want." Smith turned his palms up. "I came here to give you the first dibs on *my* coup. If you're not interested, then I overestimated your ability to see the bigger picture. I won't waste your time. I have other options."

Aikman's gaze narrowed once more. "What other options? We own this mountain. My people and yours. There's no one else."

Smith smiled. "If that's what you believe, then I really did overestimate you, Aikman."

The statement was a direct insult but it also made the other man think. "You're talking about that Hispanic gang, aren't you? They've been inching their way up the food chain for years, but they're not organized enough or financially flush enough to be more than a nuisance." He hesitated. "What is it you know that I don't?"

There was no time to go there. "We have to act fast, Aikman. We can't sit around discussing the politics of the region. Prentiss is out there looking for me right now."

Aikman scrubbed a hand over his jaw. "What is it you've got to offer?"

"You get me and my friend off this mountain and I'll give you everything you need to take down the Council. Locations, security codes. Everything. The Resurrection and all it entails will be yours for the taking."

"Where do you come back into the picture?" He shrugged. "Doesn't sound like we're doing anything. Sounds more like I'm doing and you're cutting out."

Smith shook his head. "I'll be back. There's a personal matter I have to take care of first."

Aikman grinned. "Are you referring to the woman?"

Tension slid through Smith. "I am."

Aikman scratched at his thick beard some more. "You see, that's where we have a bartering issue."

Smith's instincts stirred. "What does that mean, Aikman?"

He leaned back in his chair, his hands on the worn arms. "To tell you the truth, things get a little lonely out here from time to time. Sure there's women, but not one I've cared to take for more than a little bump and grind. There's definitely none like her. I need someone who presents a challenge. The ones I've run up on so far bore me."

Smith's gut clenched at the idea of what this bastard had in mind. The *others* were known for staying to themselves. They had no use for those who were different, whether that difference was as simple as skin color or went way deeper. The man's fascination with Buchanan would be short-lived and then she'd end up a curiosity or, worse, a sex slave.

"I don't see how that's my problem. This is business. Important business," Smith warned. "You should keep that in mind as you decide your next move."

Aikman grinned. "I'm making it your problem, Flynn. You brought this problem between you and Prentiss to my door, now I'm bringing mine to you. I want the woman. You give me the woman and we'll have a deal."

"Not happening." Smith stood. "Let's not waste each other's time with games. We'll be on our way to the next prospect if this is your final answer."

The other man stood, leaned over his desk, bracing his hands on the worn surface. "Do you really think I'm going to let you just walk back out of here?" He moved his head slowly from side to side. "This was a no-turning-back meeting, Flynn. You don't get to sit in my office and then just walk away. You think Prentiss would watch me walk away if I paid him a visit?" Aikman angled his head and studied Smith. "Then again, he might if I told him I had a gift for him. What you think you're worth to the old bastard?"

Smith smiled. "Not nearly as much as you are."

Aikman reared back, then laughed as if Smith's statement hadn't startled him. "I gave you a chance, Flynn. I guess you aren't as smart as you think. What woman is worth dying for?"

"I could ask you the same thing."

Aikman didn't flinch, but Smith saw the glimmer of uncertainty in his eyes before he blinked it away. "My people appreciate tangible proof they're being protected. With that in mind, from time to time a public display is required to keep them reassured. At dawn, we'll give them something to feel good about. Maybe the two of you will be worth all the distraction you've caused after all. You wouldn't believe what organs go for on the black market."

Smith ignored the threat, turned his back and walked out of the man's office. The guards grabbed him by the arms and jerked him forward.

Not exactly the news he'd hoped to take back to Buchanan.

SADIE HAD MOVED around the entire space and found no openings, not even a crack, except for the small round opening she'd been forced to crawl through to get in here. She couldn't help wondering if the owner of the remains in the corner had done the same thing—searched for some way to escape, wondering what would happen next—before he died here.

Whatever he'd had planned, it hadn't worked out for him.

For the first time on a mission, her mind wandered to her folks and she tried to remember the last time she'd spoken with her parents. Had she said the right things? Told them she loved them? She couldn't see her sister being there for them in their time of grief if Sadie never made it out of this place.

Don't even go there, Sadie.

Moving around the perimeter of the room once more, she closed her eyes and listened for any sort of sound. The soft whisper of words slipped beyond the crack between the stone that made a door and the hole in the wall that it covered. She couldn't say if the voices were those of the guards outside the room or people walking past in the long corridor.

The lives of these people likely revolved around the preparing and packaging of drugs. Survival. They lived to please their leader, this Aikman that Flynn asked to see. There was no logical reason why they would concern themselves with her or her survival.

Lines creased her forehead, nagging at the ache that had begun there. How long had Flynn been gone? An hour? An hour and a half? He could be dead by now for all she knew. She hugged her arms around herself, feeling oddly chilled. It would be bad enough to be stuck here with him. The concept of ending up alone in this hole—her gaze drifted across the darkness—was far worse.

Movement near the small opening drew her attention there. The rock rolled away and light poured in. Sadie stood back and waited to see what would happen. She held her breath, hoped it was Flynn and not the guards ready to drag her away to some torture chamber.

When Flynn popped up through the hole, relief rushed through her and she drew in a lungful of air.

Before he could speak, she asked, "What happened? Did you talk to Aikman?"

The stone was rolled back over the hole, blocking all but that narrow crack of light. Flynn hesitated, waiting for the guards to lose interest and wander back to their posts.

"I did. He was intrigued by my offer."

His tone told her that wasn't the whole story by any means but it might very well be the best part of it. "What was your offer?"

"The information he would need to take over the Resurrection."

No surprise there. Flynn was worried that Prentiss would get away. He didn't want that to happen. "What did you ask for in return?"

"Safe transport off this mountain."

Made sense, she supposed. If his ultimate goal was to stop Prentiss and his followers, giving away his secrets to an enemy would certainly do the trick. Not exactly the usual protocol for a federal agent, but desperate times called for desperate measures. She couldn't fault him for wanting to see his primary mission accomplished no matter that his cover was blown.

She sat down on the floor. No need to keep standing. She'd walked this space a thousand times. Exhaustion and hunger were nagging at her. "When do we leave?"

He didn't sit. Instead, he kept moving around the space as if he was agitated or frustrated. Either would be understandable under the circumstances.

"Watch for the bones on the left of the door," she warned.

Still, he said nothing, just kept moving through the near total darkness. After five minutes, his movements had grown unnerving with her sitting so still. Finally, she stood and demanded some answers. "So what's the rest of the story?"

He stopped, turned to her. She couldn't see his face, certainly couldn't read his expression, so she waited for him to explain.

"I took a calculated risk coming here. I put my offer on the table and it didn't go the way I expected."

"Can you be a little more specific?" He'd told her a considerable amount with those two statements and yet nothing at all.

"The only way he's prepared to accept my offer is if he gets *you* in the bargain."

Sadie barked out a laugh. "Are you serious?"

"Unfortunately, I am." He heaved a frustrated breath.

The idea of where they were and those bones over in the corner slammed into her midsection like a sucker punch. "How did you respond?"

On one level she could see how he might want to agree. After all, at least one of them needed to get out of here alive. It was the only way the people expecting their return would ever know what took place on this mountain. No matter that she comprehended the logic, she struggled to maintain her objectivity. Agreeing to the man's terms would be the reasonable thing to do.

At least that way Flynn could go for help. Assuming she survived whatever came after that, she could still be alive when help came.

But on a whole other level, she wanted to kick his ass for coming up with this insane idea in the first place. Fury burst through her.

As if he'd read her mind or felt her mixed emotions, he said, "I told him no way. If I go, you go."

Her heart skipped and then sank just a little. "What good does it do for both of us to be stuck here?" Or end up like the guy in the corner? She exhaled a chest full of exasperation and crossed her arms. "Tell him you changed your mind. Tell him," she added firmly, "he has a deal. You go and I'll stay."

"No way."

His hands were on his hips and she could feel his glare even if she couldn't see it.

"It's the right thing to do, Flynn. One of us needs to get down this damned mountain."

She hoped Levi Winters had found help. Maybe she would have been smarter to go with him. Except it was better that she and Flynn drew the danger away from him and let him get away. At least he could tell Ross and the others all that he knew. That was something.

"I got you into this," Flynn said, his voice low, fierce. "I'll get you out."

"How do you plan on doing that?"

He moved in closer, put his face near enough to hers that his lips brushed her ear. She shivered in spite of her best efforts not to react.

"He's not going to pass on this deal. He just wants us ready to do whatever he asks when he pretends to have a change of heart."

The feel of his breath on her skin made her want to lean into him. She pushed the idea away. "What do you think he'll want us to do?"

"He'll want us to act as a distraction while he carries out his coup."

"What kind of distraction?"

"The kind that gets captured and taken back to the compound and to Prentiss."

She jerked away from him. "What? Why the hell would we do that?"

"Because he's not a fool. He knows it won't be easy getting in even with the information I can give him. If that's what he requires, we have to be prepared to go. Are you with me?"

She wasn't so sure this plan was any better than the first one he walked in here telling her about.

But that was irrelevant.

"I'm in," she said finally. "At least we won't end up like the guy in the corner."

How had this mission turned so completely upside down?

Chapter Twelve

Tuesday, August 13

Sadie woke, her body shivering. A moment was required for her to orient herself.

Cave. Aikman. The *others*.

She sat up, scrubbed at her cheek where her face had been pressed to the cold ground. She'd been curled into a ball on the cold rock floor. She peered through the darkness, scanning the room as best she could. Listening for any sound, including breathing, she heard nothing.

Where was Flynn?

Memories of him pulling her against him in the night invaded her thoughts. She'd shivered from the cold invading her very bones and he'd pulled her against his big body to keep her warm. Several times during the night she had awakened to the feel of his protective arms around her, his shoulder like a pillow and the length of his body radiating heat into hers.

"Flynn?"

She got to her feet, dusted herself off for the good it would do. No answer. She ran her fingers through her hair. Apparently she'd slept through him being taken away.

Had Aikman summoned him for another meeting?

Her heart kicked into a faster rhythm. Maybe they'd already taken him off this damned mountain. Maybe she wasn't going anywhere.

Aikman had requested to keep her.

She chafed her arms to create some heat with the friction. Flynn would never go for it. He'd said so last night. He wasn't going without her.

Then again, it was possible he hadn't been given a choice this time.

For a few minutes she walked around, warming up her stiff, aching muscles. She really needed to use a bathroom but she doubted she would be permitted to leave her small prison. A few more minutes and she decided she couldn't wait any longer. She chose the corner the farthest away from the remains and relieved herself. The dead guy had likely been forced to do this for days or weeks before his body could no longer resist death.

Another ten or so minutes elapsed with her walking back and forth across the center of her prison cell when the stone suddenly rolled away from the opening. She moved to the wall and braced for whatever trouble might be coming. If one of the guards came in for her, she could fight him off for a while. As weary as her body was, the battle might not last long.

"Out!"

The voice was male but not one she recognized. She didn't move.

"Come out!" the man demanded. "Time to eat."

Her stomach rumbled. Getting out of here was better than staying. If it involved food, that was all the better. She pushed away from the wall and moved to the opening. On her hands and knees she scurried out as quickly as possible and shot to her feet. She didn't like being in a vulnerable position. She looked up, and two men—guards she presumed—stared down at her as if she were some sort of alien.

She blinked repeatedly to help her eyes adjust to the light. It wasn't that bright but it was a hell of a lot brighter than inside that hole she'd been stuck in all night. The two stared at her for a moment longer, then gestured for her to go to the left. Her gait was a little off at first but she soon found her rhythm. One of the guards ambled in front of her, the other behind her. They led her back the way she'd originally come into this cold, dark place. Once they were outside the cave, she squinted against the way brighter light. The sun was up but it was still early. She was escorted to one of the twig shacks and ushered through the primitive door.

A woman waited inside the shack.

"Take off your clothes and get into the tub."

She stared at Sadie, waiting for her to obey the

issued command. Her hair was long and dark like Sadie's but her skin was pale. If a bath was on the agenda, Sadie wasn't about to argue with her. She stripped off her clothes and toed off her shoes. Once she was in the tub the woman peeled the bandages from her hands and ordered her to sit. Sadie complied.

It was at precisely that moment that she considered maybe she was to be the morning kill. Maybe she was breakfast. She jerked her attention to the left just in time for a pail of water to be poured over her head. Surprisingly it was warm. A bar of soap was tossed into the tub with her and she went to work washing her face and body. It felt so good. More water poured over her and the woman started washing her hair. Sadie didn't complain. It felt amazing to have her scalp massaged. She could sit here and savor the attention for hours.

Then came more water, only this time it was cold. When she was thoroughly rinsed, the woman helped her towel off and provided a pair of blue cotton shorts and a white tee. Sadie had no idea where the clothes came from but they fit and she was glad to be out of the days-old sweats. She tugged on the same shoes she'd been wearing since her time at the compound. They were finally dry after their trek through the water. The blisters on her hands and feet were still tender but there was nothing she could do about that.

The woman ushered her over to a table and chairs and prepared food for her. The plate was metal, more like a pie tin. Scrambled eggs and toast were heaped onto the plate. A tin of water stood next to it. Sadie didn't wait to be told—she dove in. She was starving. She hoped Flynn was given food before he was taken to wherever he had gone. The food suddenly felt like a lump of cement in her stomach. She felt guilty about the nice bath and the hot food considering she had no idea where he was or what might be happening to him.

Focus, Sadie. You can't stay strong and be of any use to anyone if you don't eat.

As she forced bite after bite into her mouth, first one and then another woman came into the tiny shack and climbed into the tub of water she'd used. After five women had bathed, they shared the duty of carrying out pails of the dirty water.

Sadie understood the concept of conservation but she was immensely grateful she'd been first this morning.

The woman with the long dark hair led her back outside. One of the guards who'd escorted her from her cell was waiting. He led Sadie through the woods and to yet another shack-like house, this one larger. Once they were inside, she could see that this one was built into the mountainside and the interior was more like an actual house. A long corridor led to another door. The guard opened this door and urged her inside.

"And here she is. The woman we've been waiting for."

The man behind the desk stared at her, a grin on his face. Another man stood, rising above the chair that had prevented her from seeing him.

Flynn.

The relief that gushed through her made her knees weak. He was still here. More important, he was alive.

Rather than aim her question at Flynn, she stared directly at the other man. "What happens now?"

"Now, the two of you head out."

So Flynn had been right. This man—Aikman, she presumed—had never intended to keep her. The threat was nothing more than leverage to garner their cooperation.

"We'll take you as far as the road where you dumped the SUV. You'll be on your own from there." Aikman turned to Flynn. "As you know, I'll have eyes on you at all times. Once you're inside, I'll wait for your signal to make my move."

Sadie kept her thoughts to herself. There was no point in asking questions until she and Flynn were alone.

Flynn nodded. "On my signal."

Aikman nodded and with that gesture they were escorted from the man's office and back outside his rustic dwelling. Two all-terrain vehicles waited. One guard climbed aboard each vehicle and ordered Sadie and Flynn to do the same. Once she climbed on behind a guard and Flynn did the same with the other, a third guard dropped the black cloth bags over their heads. Aikman intended to keep their location a secret.

The vehicle bumped over roots and rocks and God only knew what else. Sadie held on tight no matter that she'd just as soon not touch the guy driving. Holding on to the enemy was better than risking a potentially fatal injury from bouncing off this rocky ride. She focused on counting off the minutes.

Half an hour later the vehicles stopped.

"Get off," the driver shouted over his shoulder at her.

Sadie reached up and removed the bag, then climbed off the ATV. The guard snatched the hood back from her as if he feared it might carry his fingerprints. She smoothed a hand over her hair as she watched the two drive away, bouncing and bumping over the terrain. When they were out of sight, she scanned the area. Woods. So thick they almost blocked the sky.

She turned to Flynn. "You're still sure about this plan?"

"I don't have an option."

She turned all the way around, surveyed the woods once more. Nothing but trees and brush. "The way I see it, we can go in whatever direction we like." Her gaze settled on him once more. "You don't have to finish this if it means you'll end up dead."

Flynn held her gaze for a long moment before he finally spoke. "You go. Stay south and you'll find your way to the main road running into Winchester.

If I still had the emergency beacon you could use that, but they took it so you'll be on your own. Keep your movements quiet and you'll be fine."

Sadie was shaking her head before he finished talking. "Either way we go, we go together."

"They have Winters," he said, his tone grave. "I have two hours to show up or he's dead."

Son of a bitch. Frustration, then fury tore through Sadie. "He should have listened to you." To both of them for that matter.

Flynn shook his head. "Doesn't matter. Prentiss had learned my identity before I left the compound with the two of you. We were never getting off this mountain without doing this or something like this."

"In that case, I guess we should get moving." Damn it all to hell. "We have a timeline we have to stick to." When he would have issued another protest, she held up her hand and shook her head.

Obviously not happy about her decision, Flynn led the way to the narrow rutted road. It split through the forest like a dusty brown snake. Sadie shuddered. She was extremely thankful they hadn't run into any creepy creatures. At least not the kind without legs.

When the silence had dragged on about as long as she could tolerate, she said, "You know, I thought you left me this morning." Might as well make conversation while they walked toward their doom.

He glanced at her. "You still don't trust me?"

"It wasn't about trust." In fact, she hadn't considered the idea of trust in a while now. She had instinctively trusted him. "I assumed you weren't given a choice. Then they took me for a bath, gave me clean clothes and fed me. The next thing I knew I was in Aikman's office with you."

His gaze traveled down the length of her, pausing on her bare legs before shifting back up to her face. "I noticed."

His attention swung back to the road. She smiled. Funny how such a simple, offhanded compliment could give her a moment's pleasure even at a time like this. But then, when you might not live beyond the next few hours it didn't take much.

As cold as she'd gotten in that cave last night, it was already hot enough to make her sweat this morning. The humidity was off the charts. Made the uphill journey even more of a slog.

Since Flynn had given her a sort of compliment, maybe she would give him one. "Thanks for keeping me warm last night." She flashed him a smile. "That was very gentlemanly of you."

"I thought you were keeping me warm."

Her jaw dropped, then he grinned. "You're a real comedian." She laughed. "Seriously, though, I appreciate it. I woke up shivering after you were gone but I remembered you keeping me warm through the night."

"You're welcome, but it was a mutual exchange."

Combined body heat. "What's going to happen when we get there?" As much as she would like to pretend they wouldn't really have to return to that damned compound, she knew there was no way around it outside the cavalry showing up out of the blue to take over the situation.

No one even knew their exact location. They were on their own and the chances of either one of them surviving were about nil. If they walked away, Levi, her target, would die. No matter that they would likely all three die anyway, she couldn't just walk away and leave him without attempting to do something. She glanced at the man beside her. She couldn't just walk away and leave Flynn to deal with this on his own, either.

"I have one sibling, a sister, and my parents." Sadie wasn't sure why she made this abrupt announcement. Just seemed like the thing to do. They might as well enjoy each other's company until they were taken prisoner again.

He said nothing for a while, just kept walking. She did the same.

"No siblings. Parents are long gone. It's just me."

So he was completely alone. "No wife or kids or best buds?"

He shook his head. "The job fills those slots."

This she understood all too well.

"Same here. Although my parents aren't going to be happy if I don't come back."

Another span of silence.

"I guess I'll have to make sure that doesn't happen."

She glanced at him again and this time he was looking back. They smiled simultaneously. It was foolish, she knew, but the shared smile had butter-flies taking flight in her stomach. "I'm sure they would appreciate that. I know I would."

The conversation waned from there. What was there to say? They both had at least a couple of choices. If they chose not to go through with this, Levi would die. If she walked away and left Flynn to go on his own and he and Levi didn't make it out, she would have to live with that decision. Levi was not Flynn's problem but he was choosing to take that responsibility. No way was she leaving him to do her job. Walking away wasn't an option.

An hour later, the road was scarcely more than a path now. They were close. Sadie remembered the terrain. The memories sent a chill over her skin. Whether it was self-preservation or utter despera-tion, she suddenly stopped.

"There has to be something else we can do." She surveyed the endless woods. "Someone who lives out here who has a phone or a vehicle."

There was no one. She was aware of this. Not any-where close by at any rate. Still, she couldn't *not* ask the question again. Being ambushed was one thing but walking into a death trap was just plain crazy. Of course, that was exactly what she'd done to get into the compound in the first place.

What did that say about the two of them? Maybe they both had death wishes that they explained away with their careers.

"There's no one for miles." He stopped walking

and turned to face her. "I understood the risk when I started this. There's no way out."

Sadie moved in on him, taking the three steps between them. "Are you doing this for you or for your father?"

He looked away from her but not before she saw emotions cloud his eyes. "Does it matter?"

She folded her arms over her chest to prevent reaching out to him. One of her instructors had warned her about a place exactly like this. The place you find yourself when you've lost all sight of the difference between your life and your work. When work becomes more important than anything else— even surviving.

"This is the job, Flynn. This isn't about you or your father. This is the job. Justice. Doing the right thing. Taking down the bad guys for the greater good, not for your own personal reasons. Like maybe revenge."

He laughed, shook his head. "Did you spend the last hour thinking up that speech or did you suddenly remember it from your agent-in-training handbook?"

She had definitely hit a nerve. "Don't be a smart-ass. I'm only trying to help. To make you see that we've both lost sight of what we were trained to do. What we swore to do when we started this journey."

"I don't need a lecture, and the only way you can help is to walk down that mountain to safety while I do what I have to do."

Now he was just being arrogant. "Levi Winters

is my target. He's my responsibility. I have just as much right to walk into this trap as you do."

He stared at her long and hard. "It's only a trap if you don't see it coming."

"We need a plan, Flynn. We shouldn't just walk into this, whatever you want to call it, without a plan."

"I have a plan."

That was the moment she remembered what Aikman said. The memory had rocks forming in her gut. "What did your friend mean when he said he would wait for your signal?"

"Let's go."

When he would have turned to start walking again, she grabbed him by the arm. "We're in too deep for you to blow me off at this stage of the game."

He stared at her, his own anger blazing in his eyes.

"It means just what he said, I give the signal, he and his people invade. I've given them the access codes along with the guard locations. Now let's get moving."

Did he really think she was going to let it go? "What's the signal?"

Since they didn't have a cell phone, beacon, flare gun, air horn or any damned thing else, just how the hell did he expect to give anyone outside the compound a signal?

The stare-off continued. Ten seconds, fifteen, twenty.

Enough. She made up her mind then and there. She grabbed him by the shirtfront and jerked his face down to hers. Then she kissed him. Kissed him hard on the mouth. Kept her lips pressed to his until he reacted. His fingers plowed into her hair and pulled her more firmly into him, deepening the kiss, taking control.

She poured herself into the kiss, into the feel of his mouth, his lips and his palms against her face. When the need for air forced them apart, he looked her straight in the eye and said, "I'm still not telling you."

The answer to the question was suddenly as clear as shiny new glass. He had no way of sending a signal.

"They have someone inside, don't they? That's the person who'll give the signal when you've done whatever it is Aikman has asked of you."

He looked away.

She shook her head. "All this time they've had someone inside. Why the hell do they need you?"

"We're running out of time. Let's go."

She grabbed him by the forearm, kept him from turning away. "No. Not until you tell me the truth."

Fury tightened the lips she had only moments ago kissed. Wanted to kiss again, damn her.

"You don't have a need to know, Agent Buchanan."

A sharp laugh burst out of her. "Don't even try playing that game with me." She held his gaze, silently demanding an answer. She saw the answer without him having to say a word. The determination as well as the resignation. Her heart stumbled. "You're going to kill Prentiss, aren't you? That's the signal Aikman will be waiting for."

He snapped his gaze away from hers and started to walk once more, but not before she saw the defeat in his eyes.

Prentiss's bodyguards would kill Flynn.

There was no way he would survive.

She had to figure out a way to turn this around.

Chapter Thirteen

Smith started walking. He could not allow her to sway his decision. She didn't understand. Aikman would have killed her after doing other unspeakable things if Smith hadn't agreed to his terms.

There was no other choice. No way out.

It was true that at this moment there was some measure of leeway. Quite possibly they could take off and maybe get down this damned mountain before they were caught. But that would be like putting a gun to Levi Winters's head and pulling the trigger. If that wasn't bad enough, Prentiss would no doubt disappear.

This—right now—was the one chance Smith had of stopping him.

"You're a fool."

He ignored her, which wasn't easy to do. She had surprised him when she kissed him. He'd felt the mutual attraction almost from the beginning, couldn't have missed it if he'd tried. The intensity of it was his own fault. It had been way too long since he'd allowed himself basic human pleasures. She made him want to indulge those ignored needs. It was difficult for a starving man to ignore a buffet right in front of him.

"This goes against your training. We both understand what needs to happen. This is a textbook example of a no-win situation. We need backup."

"You feel strongly about following the rules, is that it, Buchanan?" She was as bad as him. She'd walked into a deadly situation without so much as a blink and damned sure without any backup. She had no right to judge his actions.

"It's not the same," she argued.

"It's exactly the same."

She stopped and turned to him. He bumped into her shoulder.

"I didn't walk into that compound prepared to kill a man."

Anger clenched his jaw. He struggled to utter an answer. She couldn't possibly understand. "He deserves to die."

She nodded. "Maybe so but not because you want to put a bullet in his brain. What you're talking about is premeditated murder. Are you a murderer, Flynn?"

He bit his lips together to prevent denying the charge. Maybe he was a murderer. He had never wanted to kill another man the way he wanted to kill Prentiss.

"If you are, what makes you any better than him?"

A part of him wanted to refute her words. To explain his reasoning. But did any of it really matter? He wanted to watch Rayford Prentiss die. He couldn't wait to see him take his last breath. Equally important, he wanted the bastard to know that he—Smith Flynn, the son of Avery Flynn—had been the one to bring his ruthless reign and his life to an end.

"Nothing," he admitted.

He walked on. They were close to the compound. The watchers would spot them and send out a team to bring them in. It wouldn't be long now.

The answer he'd given to her last question kept her quiet for a few minutes. She was searching for some other rationalization for why he couldn't do what Aikman had ordered him to do. He could practically hear the wheels in her head turning. She wanted to help him.

But she couldn't.

No one could. Not at this point. It was too late.

As much as he regretted what he had become and all the things he'd had to do, if necessary he would do it all again to stop Prentiss.

"Once we're inside, give me some time," she suddenly said, her voice low as if she feared the trees had ears. Most likely they did.

"Time for what?" He asked this without looking at her. He didn't want to look at her. Not simply because she was attractive and alluring and made him want things he shouldn't. But because she reminded him of all that was good—of the reason he became an agent in the first place. She made him want the career he'd had before this journey started. She made him wish things had been different.

Could he be that man again? Did the good part of him even still exist? He had worked for two long years to erase that guy. To make him immune to the emotions that would only get in his way.

Buchanan had made a valid point. He was a murderer. He'd killed the man he used to be. What he was now was no better than Prentiss.

He doubted there was any going back.

She stopped again, moved in close to him, making his body yearn to pull her close. "Once we're inside, give me time to create a distraction. We can turn this around, Flynn, make it work for us."

The hope in her eyes made him want to believe her. Made him want to grab on to the life raft she offered and hang on for the ride.

But what if she was wrong?

"He won't be fooled so easily this time. He knows he can't trust either of us. How do you expect to manipulate him in any way to buy time or anything else?"

She was an optimist. A woman who wanted to stand by the goodness and justice she believed in. She needed him to believe, too, but he'd lost the ability to blindly believe in anything.

"Trust me, Flynn. You would be surprised at the tricks I have up my sleeve."

He shouldn't agree to the idea. He should do what he had to do and be grateful for the opportunity.

But she made him want to do the right thing.

"I'll give you as much time as I can."

She grinned. "That's all I can ask for, partner."

Despite the worry and uncertainty nagging at him, he smiled back at her. Maybe they could turn this around.

He just hoped she lived through it. He had never expected to survive this assignment, but he didn't want to be the reason she lost her life.

As they ascended the next ridge, troops came out of the trees. Seven, no eight. The group swarmed out and surrounded their position, weapons leveled on his and Buchanan's heads.

Smith held perfectly still. "I need to see Prentiss."

"He doesn't want to see you."

Smith knew this soldier. He was an ambitious man. He would want to prove he was somehow responsible for Smith's capture.

"Take me to him," he said to the younger man, daring him to argue. Smith was now listed as an enemy but there would be those who had their doubts. Those who feared turning their backs on him since it was not out of the question that he could be restored to his former position. After all, he was Avery Flynn's only son.

The soldier gave a nod to one of his minions. "Search them both."

When he and Buchanan had been patted down to the man's satisfaction, he ordered his team to move out. The soldiers stayed in a tight ring around Smith and Buchanan as they continued on to the compound.

The compound was only a mile or so away at this point. He glanced at Buchanan. Somehow he had to find a way to keep her from ending up dead no matter that she refused to cooperate.

She'd asked for time, which likely meant she had a plan. Maybe he should listen to her reasoning. She wasn't emotionally tangled up with this situation and he was. Her reasoning might be clearer than his own. He'd been guilty of a lot of mistakes over the years but he didn't have to make one today.

PRENTISS WAITED ALONE in the meeting room.

Of course he wouldn't want any of the other members of the Council present when he said what he had to say. The secrets and lies he had kept over all these years were not the sort he wanted anyone to know, particularly those who looked to him to lead them. There was not a bigger con artist alive. The man was capable of anything if it gained him what he wanted. But the other members of the Council, the followers, none of them would ever believe he was anything other than a selfless leader who protected their way of life.

Smith had barely resisted the urge to take a swing at one of the guards when he prepared to separate Buchanan from him. As two guards dragged her away she had shouted for him to remember what she said.

He did remember.

For what it was worth, he would try his best to give her some time.

Smith was shackled and escorted to a chair, where he was forced to sit before the shackles around his ankles were anchored to the floor. Prentiss didn't speak until the guards had left the room. Only the two of them would ever know the whole story if Prentiss had his way.

"Is it true?" the old man asked as if he could hardly believe the reality of what had occurred.

"What would you know about the truth?" Looking at him sickened Smith. How had he managed these past two years?

"I know enough," Prentiss warned. "I know a mole when I see one. A traitor. A man whose entire existence is a betrayal to his own people."

"Doesn't matter now," Smith mused, deciding on a delay tactic that might just work. "You're finished."

The old man's gaze narrowed. "I don't believe you. If the feds had anything on me, they would be here now arresting me and pinning medals on you." He glanced around the room. "I don't see or hear anyone coming to your rescue. Perhaps you should pray about this dilemma in which you find yourself."

Smith chuckled. "I don't need to pray, old man. I've spent two years feeding information to those feds. They have what they need, they're only waiting for the perfect moment. Believe me when I say that moment is close at hand."

"If that's true, then why were you and your friend still wandering about on this mountain? Why haven't your comrades rescued you? Or have they forsaken you as you have forsaken me?"

"I refused a rescue. I want to watch from right here." He smiled. "I want to witness them dragging you away in shackles." He shook his head. "Too bad the other members of the Council are going down with you. They are only guilty of following your orders. How fast do you think one or more of them will roll over and start spilling his guts about the executions and the shipments?"

Prentiss stood and moved toward him. He looked even older and more than a little frail in those overalls and worn boots. But there was nothing frail about this bastard. He was dangerous. Ruthless. Cunning as hell.

"I will know what you've told them," he warned as he braced his hands on the arms of the chair and leaned in close to Smith. "I will know every secret and every name you've shared. And then you will die a slow, agonizing death."

Smith allowed a wide smile to slide across his lips once more. "I shared them all. Every single name, every single secret. They know about your partners in South America. They know your next incoming shipment and the distribution channels you intend to use. They know *everything*."

"I want names," Prentiss demanded. "Who are your contacts?"

"You can't stop this, old man. They're coming and you and all this will fall."

Prentiss drew back sharply as if he feared catching some contagious disease. "Your father would be sickened by your actions. He would kill you himself."

Smith leaned forward as far as his shackles would allow. "My father was not like you. He would be grateful to me for stopping you."

Prentiss held his ground. "Maybe you're right. Avery had grown weak in his old age. He failed to see what was best for the security of our people. Progress is necessary. As is extending our reach. He was blind to those needs."

"But they followed him. Looked up to him. Not you," Smith reminded him. "You were always in his shadow."

Prentiss was the one smiling then. "And yet I'm still here and he is gone."

"How much longer do you think you can hang on when your people learn you failed to see the traitor in their midst? Or maybe they'll see you as the traitor."

"They already know what you are. You're just like your father. Weak. Shortsighted. A stumbling block to survival."

Anger ignited deep inside Smith. "My father was not weak. His vision was far greater than yours. You will never be half the leader he was."

"Before I order your public execution perhaps it's time you were told what really happened."

Smith stilled. His father suffered a heart attack. "I'm well aware of how he died."

On some level he would always believe that his decision to leave had been part of the burden that weighed upon his father, making him a prime candidate for a sudden heart attack. He couldn't help wondering if he'd secretly discovered what Smith had become, a traitor to all his father believed.

"His heart stopped true enough." Prentiss reared back, his thumbs hooked into the side splits of his overalls. "It was the only way to protect what we had achieved. He would have ruined everything."

Something cold and dark swelled inside Smith. "What does that mean?"

"It means," the bastard said, obviously enjoying the moment, "that he wanted to pull back. When he found out about my deal with the cartel, he demanded I leave. He intended to put me out after I had dedicated my life to the cause." Prentiss shrugged. "It was him or me. He was too sick to understand what he was saying and doing. So, as you can see, it wasn't me."

Shock radiated through Smith. "You killed him?"

"I did," Prentiss confessed. "Just like I'm going to kill you."

SADIE DIDN'T BOTHER STRUGGLING. Prentiss had ordered her to the tunnels. Her friend Levi, Prentiss had warned, was already there, unless he'd ended up as dinner earlier than expected.

No wonder Flynn wanted to kill the man. He was a ruthless degenerate. Every minute he drew breath, someone else suffered.

The dome was pulled back by one of her guards, revealing the ladder that led deep under the ground. Sadie went along, feigning uncertainty. She had a plan and having it start in the tunnels would work to her advantage.

When she reached the bottom of the ladder, George was waiting. He still wore those flimsy flip-flops he'd bartered out of her.

"Wasn't expecting you back," he said. "I heard you ran off."

"I missed you and decided to drop by for a visit."

He stared at her a long moment, her light sarcasm seemingly lost on him. Finally, he nodded. "Anyway, your friend is down here, too. He ain't faring so well."

"What's wrong with him?"

"I guess he don't like the idea that if an emergency happens and we run out of food, he'll be the backup."

Levi was supplies. Prentiss had enjoyed telling her that, as well. Before George could turn and start walking away, she said, "We should probably talk before joining the others."

He frowned. "You know the drill down here. What do we have to talk about?"

Sadie looked around as if to make sure no one else was nearby. "They're coming today. If all of you are still here, you'll end up in jail, too."

Confusion flashed in his eyes. "Who's coming?"

"The feds, local law enforcement. They're coming to take Prentiss and the Council to jail. They know everything about this place."

He shrugged. "They've boasted about taking Prentiss down before and it never happens. He's way too careful."

"Trust me, George. I'm with the FBI. They know everything. You were nice to me so I'd like to help you and the others down here. But there isn't a lot of time. We should get out of here while we still can."

"What?" He drew back as if her words had attacked him.

"You know how to get out. You've dug egress routes. You know where they are and how to use them. Don't pretend you don't, George."

"I think we should get to work." He started walking deeper into the tunnel.

Sadie didn't move. She stayed next to the ladder. She wasn't going anywhere until she got George thinking about how easy it would be to escape this tunnel and flee to someplace well beyond the reach of the Resurrection. Not that the group would have any power left when this was done. She decided on a new tactic.

"Prentiss and the rest of the Council are leaving. You think they're going to let you guys out of here before they evacuate?" She shook her head. "They'll leave you to die. The authorities can't question the dead."

He stalled, shook his head at her. "You're lying."

"I'm not lying, George. I have no reason to lie. I just don't want to die and that's what will happen if we don't get out of here."

He started walking again. She followed.

"The feds are coming to take Prentiss and his Council down. They'll be here before nightfall. We don't have time to waste. Prentiss and his cronies are going to get away clean and all of us down here won't."

He stopped and glanced back at her again. "If what you're saying is true, what do you expect us to do?"

"You told me about the egresses you've prepared. Let's go to the closest one and get out of here before it's too late. Before Prentiss orders any and all loose ends cleaned up."

"There will be guards waiting at the egresses," he argued. "They'll shoot us."

She shook her head. "They'll be gone. They're afraid. They're not going to hang around once word about what's coming gets around."

George kept moving until he reached the work area. Sadie trudged along behind him. Levi was there and he looked in reasonably good condition. No visible injuries. Relief rushed through her. Maybe this would be a second chance to get him safely out of here. This time she wasn't allowing him out of her sight. She fully intended to deliver him to his sister.

With his shovel in his hand, George joined the

others. Sadie wanted to shake him. Why the hell wasn't he listening? She needed something to happen soon if she was going to help Smith.

"Hey," she shouted at him. "Didn't you hear what I said? We have to get out of here or we're all going to die. Why aren't you telling these people?"

Several of the men glanced at her and then at George but made no move to stop what they were doing.

"Levi!" She waited for him to look at her. "Come on. We're getting out of here."

He looked around at the other men. Just when Sadie was certain he would keep working, he threw down his shovel and walked toward her.

Another wave of relief swept through her. "Who else is with us?"

She scanned the dirty faces. All stared at her, their expressions weary, defeated.

"Tell them, George," she urged. "Tell them what's about to happen up there. We have to run while we still can."

George stared at her for a long moment, then he threw down his pickax and stalked toward her. She held her breath, not certain whether he intended to yank her over to take his place or if he intended to join her.

When he reached her, he turned back to the others. "We'll need shovels and axes. It'll take us at least twenty minutes and if they see us on the cameras, they'll come down here and make us wish we hadn't listened to her."

"We can do this," Sadie urged, not wanting his warning to dissuade them. "We'll work faster than we ever have before."

George surveyed the men now watching him. "Grab your shovels and the axes. We're out of here."

Much to her immense gratitude, George led the way. Sadie and Levi followed. At least twelve more hustled along the corridor behind them. She glanced at the cameras placed overhead approximately every fifteen yards along the seemingly endless corridor. They wouldn't have a lot of time.

The alarm was sounding by the time they reached the closest egress. Six of the men climbed the ladders and started to dig. Six more formed a wall across the tunnel in anticipation of the guards who would no doubt come.

The sound of boots pounding on the ground echoed through the tunnel. George and his friends were shouting at each other to hurry. Sadie dragged Levi closer.

"As soon as that egress is cleared," she murmured close to his ear, "we have to get out of here and go for help."

He nodded his understanding.

Shouting in the tunnel echoed some ten yards away.

Hurry. Sadie looked from the wall of bodies

standing between the coming guards and their position to the men jabbing and poking overhead.

"Go!"

Sadie jerked her attention toward George. Sunlight suddenly poured into the tunnel. Three of the men were already scrambling out.

"Let's go." Sadie nudged Levi forward.

They rushed up the ladders and climbed out. Two guards who had been taking a smoke break suddenly turned toward them. George and the others were on top of them before they could get their weapons into position.

Others were clambering out behind Sadie and Levi.

Sadie didn't look back. She held on to Levi's hand and ran through the woods as fast as she could.

She had no idea how far they were from help but she had to get to wherever that was as quickly as possible.

Smith's life depended upon it.

Chapter Fourteen

Sadie kept a firm grasp on Levi's hand as they ran through the woods, branches and undergrowth slapping at her bare legs.

The crack of gunfire behind them forced Sadie's heart into a faster cadence.

She charged forward with a new burst of adrenaline-inspired speed. Levi managed to keep up though he was barefoot and stumbling with exhaustion. He would pay for the lack of shoes or boots later. She imagined he had blisters on his hands just as she'd had after her time in the tunnel, though hers were partially healed now.

If the guards got off a good shot, the two of them would have far more than blisters to worry about.

"This way." Levi tugged at the hand she had clenched around his.

He knew the area and she didn't. She might as well trust him. He had as much reason to want to escape this mountain as she did. Staying alive was always a strong motivator no matter which side of the equation one was on.

Levi deviated into a different direction. Plowed through the jungle of trees.

By the time they slowed Sadie could barely get her breath.

"Hold on a minute." Levi leaned against a tree and struggled to catch his breath, as well.

Sadie propped against the nearest tree and took slow, deep breaths. When she could string words together, she asked, "How far to civilization?"

"If we keep going this way—" he hitched a thumb in the direction they'd been headed, south Sadie thought "—we'll hit the valley in about a mile and a half. There are a few houses in that area. We can probably use a phone there."

Sadie nodded. Worked for her.

When they headed out again they moved considerably slower. Sadie's muscles burned from the hard run and the abuse they'd suffered the past several days. She would need weeks to recover from the way she'd mistreated her body on this mission.

Assuming she survived. She glanced over her shoulder to ensure no one was coming. Clear for now.

As they moved downward the underbrush grew less dense. Even the trees weren't so thick. Up ahead beyond the tree line an open pasture came into view. She and Levi hesitated at the edge of the woods to have a look at what lay beyond.

Sadie spotted a house and barn in the distance.

Judging by the cows in the field and the farm equipment scattered about, someone lived there. There were other houses beyond that one. Acres of open pasture rolled out between the houses. She glanced behind her once more. Moving through those open areas would be risky if the enemy on their trail caught up with them.

Sadie turned to the man at her side. "Do you know any of the people who live on this stretch of road?"

Levi shook his head. "All we need is to use the phone, right? Surely one of them will let us do that whether they know us or not."

Sadie nodded. "We'll tell them our car broke down. If we mention the trouble on our heels, they may not let us in the house. Some people don't like to get involved."

"Yeah." He surveyed the expanse of green space in front of them. "You're right. We can't tell them what's really going on."

Sadie scanned the woods behind them. She listened for several seconds. "Maybe we lost those guards."

More than a dozen people had escaped the tunnel. Most went in different directions. Hopefully, the two guards she had spotted as well as those who had come up from the tunnel had followed some of the others. Not that she wished that unlucky break on anyone, but she was only human.

"Let's try that first house," she suggested. "The sooner we get to town the sooner we can send help for Flynn." Her stomach twisted at the idea that he could be dead already. She had urged him to buy some time. To do his best to drag out the inevitable. She hoped he was successful. As long as he didn't allow his emotions to take over, he would be okay. He was a well-trained agent. Hopefully that training would kick in and keep him thinking smart.

With one last backward glance, she and Levi dashed across the pasture. Part of her braced for the crack of a weapon firing at them but it didn't come. As they neared the house a cow raised its head and stared at them.

They bounded up onto the front porch. Levi reached the door first. He knocked. Sadie kept a watch on the tree line to ensure no one came rushing out after them. All they needed was a phone. One call.

Her pulse pounded as Levi knocked again. No television sound, no footsteps moving about. The house sounded empty. Worried that was indeed the case, Sadie peered through the nearest window. *Kitchen.* There were drying dishes on a towel on the counter. If no one was home now, they had been earlier.

"Somebody lives here." She checked the tree line and pasture again.

A loud thump drew her attention to the door. Levi backed up and body-slammed it again, using his right shoulder.

Sadie winced as he slammed it a third time before it gave way and burst inward.

She exhaled a big breath and followed him across the threshold. Breaking and entering wasn't such a bad thing considering they were running for their lives.

"Phone's over here," Levi said.

Sadie went to the side table beneath the big front window. "Have a look around and make sure no one's in the shower or something. We don't need an armed homeowner thinking we mean harm to him or his property."

She sure as hell didn't want to escape armed killers only to end up shot by a terrified farmer or his wife.

Levi nodded and headed into the hall. The house was a brick rancher, not so large. It wouldn't take him long to have a look.

Sadie entered 911 into the handset. As soon as the dispatcher finished her spiel, she identified herself and asked to be connected to Sheriff Tanner.

Tanner was on the line in under twenty seconds.

Sadie sagged with relief. "Tanner, we're..." Hearing footsteps, she turned to ask Levi exactly where they were.

Gun.

She froze.

Levi stood in the cased opening between the living room and the hall, his hands high in the air. An older man wearing a cap had the business end of a rifle jammed into the side of his head. Levi's eyes were round with fear.

"I tried to tell him we need help," Levi explained.

"Put the phone down," the man demanded.

Damn. "Sir, I'm on the phone with Sheriff Tanner." She thrust the phone at the man. "We're unarmed. Speak to the sheriff and he'll explain everything."

The man backed away from Levi but kept a bead on his head. He took the cordless phone receiver from Sadie and backed a few steps farther away in order to keep them both in his line of vision.

"Sheriff Tanner, this is Cord Hawkins." Hawkins gave the address and then listened as Tanner spoke.

Sadie couldn't make out what he was saying but she heard the rumble of his voice. Judging by the way the man lowered the barrel of his weapon, he understood Sadie and Levi were no threat to him.

"I'll do it," Hawkins said. He offered the receiver to Sadie. "Sheriff wants to talk to you again."

"Thank you." Sadie took the phone and pressed it to her ear. "Tell me you're on your way. We don't have much time."

As Tanner passed along orders via another phone line, Sadie was vaguely aware that Hawkins had brought cans of cola from the kitchen. He passed one to Levi and offered one to her.

Sadie summoned a smile and murmured a thank-you. She popped the top and downed half the can before Tanner turned his attention back to the conversation with her.

"Sit tight, Agent Buchanan, we're on our way to you. We'll have that mountain covered within the hour."

Sadie ended the call and drank more of the cola. Levi leaned against the wall and slid to the floor as he guzzled his cola. Sadie closed her eyes against the weariness dragging at her. She had never been so tired in her life.

"Are those friends of yours?"

Sadie jerked her attention back to the here and now and rushed across the room to the big window. Hawkins pointed at three men running across the same pasture she and Levi had sprinted across. She peered across the distance to make out their faces. One was George, she decided. She didn't need to recognize the faces of the other two. All wore the dirty sweats and sported the greasy hair and dirty faces of tunnel workers.

"They were prisoners just like us." She turned to Hawkins. "They're not the bad guys."

His fingers tightened around his rifle. "You sure about that, ma'am?"

She nodded. "I'll go out and talk to them."

"I'll be watching," Hawkins assured her.

"Thank you."

Sadie stepped out the front door as the three men bounded up the porch steps. "Did they follow you?" She hadn't seen anyone else coming out of that tree line.

George shook his head. "We lost them."

"Hurry." Sadie opened the door. "Let's get inside. The sheriff is on the way with help."

Hawkins passed out colas to the three and dug up a couple of big bags of chips. The men ate as if they hadn't eaten in days. Probably hadn't. She kept her attention on the tree line and said a prayer for Flynn.

He was still at that compound. On his own.

"The sheriff's here," Hawkins announced.

A whole parade of official vehicles arrived. Uniformed deputies and officers poured into the house. Paramedics insisted on giving Sadie, Levi and the other three a quick check while she and George provided information about the compound, the people there and the precarious position in which they'd left Agent Smith Flynn.

Winchester's chief of police, William Brannigan, was already on the phone with the ATF. The state police and the Bureau had been notified en route. Through the window Sadie spotted Agent Ross and Cece Winters, coming up the porch steps.

"Levi." Sadie turned to the young man who had resumed his seat on the floor. "Someone's here for you."

He pushed to his feet at the same time that his sister and Ross entered the house. The reunion of brother and sister was the one good thing that had happened this day. Sadie was grateful to be a part of it.

Cece Winters hugged Sadie next. "Thank you for rescuing my brother."

Sadie glanced at Levi. "I think it was a mutual rescue."

He smiled. "Maybe."

Special Agent Deacon Ross shook Sadie's hand. "I appreciate what you must have gone through to make this happen."

"We're not finished yet," she warned. "There's a war about to happen on that mountain. The Resurrection and the *others* are going head-to-head. Agent Flynn is caught in the middle of it. He could be dead already. We have to hurry."

George suddenly stepped forward. "I know the one access road to get to that compound. Know the codes, too. I'll take you there."

The other two who had come with George echoed his offer.

They all wanted to see Prentiss go down.

No one wanted that more than Sadie.

"Ms. Winters will take you back to my office," Tanner said to Sadie.

She shook her head. "No way. I'm going with you."

Tanner started to argue but he must have seen the absolute determination in Sadie's eyes. He nodded. "All right, then, let's move out."

SMITH STRUGGLED TO FOCUS.

He hung from a hook attached to the ceiling, his feet dangling several inches off the floor. He'd been stripped to the waist and tortured for hours. He'd lost track of the time.

The beating he rode out without much more than a flinch. The shock torture had become tedious the last half hour or so. This was nothing he hadn't endured before. But it was the burns that were about to be inflicted with a branding iron he would just as soon skip.

Prentiss, the son of a bitch, watched from a safe distance across the room as the irons turned red amid the fiery coals. Smith knew the soldier tasked with the job of inflicting the torture. The man didn't appear to feel bad about having to torture an old friend. Maybe Smith had made more enemies than he'd realized during his time here. Or maybe the guy was just glad to be the one inflicting the torture and not the one receiving it.

Who could blame him?

The one thing Smith knew with absolute certainty was that providing he survived long enough he would kill Rayford Prentiss if it was the last thing he ever did.

The bastard had admitted to murdering his father.

Prentiss was responsible for the deaths of countless other people with his gunrunning and drug trade. And that was only the beginning.

As if his thoughts had summoned him, Prentiss dared to venture closer. He surveyed Smith, enjoying the blood dribbling from his mouth and nose, the swelling of his face and eyes as well as the bruises forming on his torso. All these things gave him pleasure. This bastard had tortured and murdered many. But Smith would be his last, one way or another.

Whether Smith survived this day or not, Buchanan would ensure the bastard got what he deserved.

If she had survived.

Smith closed his eyes against any other possibility. She was too smart and too determined to fail. Prentiss had been called out of the room once, a couple of hours ago. Smith hadn't been able to hear all that was said but he'd picked up on the gist of the conversation. There had been an escape. Ten or twelve people had dug out of the tunnel and evaded the posted guards.

She would be one of them, Smith felt certain.

Go, Sadie.

A smile tugged at his damaged lips. He liked her name. *Sadie.* He liked her sassiness and her courage.

He hoped he had the chance to get to know her better.

"What on God's green earth do you have to smile about, boy?"

Smith opened his swollen eyes as best he could. "I was just thinking how you'll rot in prison with all your friends. Oh wait." He managed a rusty laugh. "You don't have any friends. That should be interesting."

He'd expected Aikman to show up even though he didn't get a signal indicating Smith had taken care of Prentiss. With all the access codes and information Smith had provided him, he'd figured the man would make a move either way.

"I thought maybe you were worried about your own friend, or enemy as the case might be," Prentiss said. "Aikman, I believe his name is."

Smith clenched his aching jaw to prevent showing a reaction to the name.

"You see, I found out about his man inside. He was watching, nosing around in places he didn't belong today, so I guessed something was up. Unlike you, he sang like a bird with very little prodding. My people are on high alert. No one is getting into this compound today or any other. Strange." He rubbed at his beard. "I understand you were going to kill me. Whatever changed your mind?"

Smith smiled again, his split lip burning like fire. "I decided I'd rather know that you're rotting in a prison cell than give you an easy way out. I want you to live, old man. A very long time so you can enjoy what the future holds for you when justice is served."

Prentiss picked up one of the knives lying on the table with all the other torture instruments. He turned it over in his hand, pretending to inspect the stainless steel blade and handle.

Tension slid through Smith. He braced to lift his

legs and kick him across the room. He'd been waiting for time alone with the guy administering the torture in hopes of using that move as a means to escape, but so far that moment hadn't come. Once he attempted any sort of maneuver, if he was unsuccessful steps would be taken to ensure he was unable to repeat the effort. So he had waited. Unfortunately, his strength was waning far too quickly. He'd have to make a move soon or find himself unable to do so.

The door on the other side of the room opened and one of Prentiss's private bodyguards rushed in. He whispered something in the old man's ear. Prentiss set the knife aside. His gaze settled on Smith as he listened to the rest of what the man had to say.

It was happening. Smith didn't have to hear the words. He saw the abrupt fear in the old man's eyes.

Prentiss looked to the other man in the room. "Finish him and clear out."

Oh yeah. Either Aikman and his people were descending on the compound or the backup Sadie had gone after was close.

Either option suited Smith.

Prentiss hurried out with his bodyguard.

Smith held very still as the man who'd beat and tortured him walked toward him for the last time. Mentally preparing himself to expend the last of his physical strength, Smith waited until the man was close enough to pick up that big-ass knife from the table. His fingers wrapped around the handle and he weighed it, hoping to add a layer of tension, to build the dread.

Smith made his move.

He wrapped his legs around the man's neck and squeezed. Struggling to free himself, the bastard lifted his right hand, aiming the knife at Smith.

Smith used his whole body to jerk to the right, snapping the bastard's neck. His eyes bulged. The knife fell from his slack fingers and clanged on the floor. Smith loosened his hold and the now-lifeless body followed that route, dropping like a rock.

Swinging his legs to the left, Smith grabbed hold of the table with his bare feet. He hung that way for a moment to catch his breath and to give his muscles a moment to recover. Slowly, he used his feet to drag the table closer. When he could kneel on it, he rested another moment. Finally, he pushed upward, lifting his bound hands from the meat hook that had held him suspended in the air. He collapsed into a kneeling position on the table. A few minutes were required for his arms to stop stinging.

He scooted off the table and found his footing on the floor. Where the hell was the key to these wrist shackles? He checked the table and the items that had been flung to the floor when he'd dragged it close. No key. Then he checked the dead guy who'd wielded the hours of torture. The key was in his right front pocket. Smith pulled the key free.

Collapsing into a cross-legged position, he focused on getting the key into the lock that held an iron bracelet around his left wrist. He dropped the key, once, twice before he managed to get it into the lock. He had to twist his right hand in an awkward position to turn the key but he finally managed. The lock on his left wrist fell open. Relief surged through him. He picked up the key and unlocked the bracelet on his right wrist. When the final shackle fell free, he rubbed his wrists and dragged in a deep breath. His damaged ribs ached with the move.

Pushing to his feet, he surveyed the room for a weapon.

Depending on who had arrived, he could be in for another battle for his life. He turned over the dead guy, snatched the gun from his waistband. He checked the ammo cartridge. Full. He shoved the gun into his waistband and went in search of his shoes. He finally found them in a pile with the shirt that had been cut from his body. The shirt he could live without but the shoes would be useful.

Now to find Prentiss before the bastard managed to slip away.

Smith stalled halfway to the door and went back to the dead guy for his cell phone. It was possible Prentiss would call to ensure Smith was dead. He no doubt wanted Smith dead as badly as Smith wanted him caught. A vehicle fob fell out of the guy's pocket. Smith took that, as well.

Running footsteps in the corridor outside the door snapped Smith's attention in that direction. He started toward the door. Halfway across the room it opened.

Smith leveled the weapon on the potential threat.

Aikman.

Chapter Fifteen

"Well, well, if it isn't the man who failed his mission." Aikman shook his head. "*Tsk, tsk*, Flynn, I had you pegged for better than that."

Apparently the idea that Smith was the one holding the gun aimed at him didn't faze the guy. Aikman's weapon was in his hand but not aimed at anything other than the floor. Whoever else had been in that corridor with him had moved on to the next door. A bad decision any way you looked at it.

"I was working on it and the bastard found out you had invaded the compound. So he took off while I was still a little tied up."

Aikman glanced at the meat hook beyond Smith. "Ouch."

Smith wasn't sure whether the guy was trying to put him off-balance or if he really wasn't worried about the weapon aimed at his head just now.

"You might want to put that weapon away," Smith suggested. "I don't want to get nervous and do something we'll both regret."

Aikman smiled, made a laugh/grunt sound. "Of course." He tucked the weapon into his waistband. "We've decided we prefer these accommodations over our own. So we'll be taking over the compound."

"You planning on killing everyone here?" Smith hoped like hell backup was close.

Aikman shrugged. "There are some I'd rather have join my team." He made a questioning face. "You interested, Flynn?"

He lowered his weapon and wiped his bleeding mouth. "Why not? As long as the terms are agreeable."

Aikman glanced around the room. "Where's your little friend? I was looking forward to seeing her again."

"I'd like to know the answer to that one myself." He started toward the door that Aikman currently blocked. "I'm hoping Prentiss didn't take her with him." Smith knew that wasn't the case but Aikman couldn't know.

Aikman turned his back to Smith and exited the room first. The guy continued to surprise Smith.

"We've rounded up all the Council members." Aikman glanced at him as they moved along the corridor. "Except Prentiss and you, of course."

Dread thickened in Smith's gut. "Did you kill them?"

Aikman shook his head. "Not yet. They no doubt have information I'll need going forward. Unless you have everything you think we'll need. In that case we can be rid of them right away."

"Prentiss was careful never to give all the power to one person. Each of us had our domain. We'll need them all."

This was a lie but if it kept Aikman from performing a mass execution, that was all that mattered.

There was just one problem as far as Smith could see. He couldn't be sure which of the Council members would be smart enough to keep his mouth shut about him being an undercover agent. If any of those who knew warned Aikman, this situation would do a one-eighty in a heartbeat.

He needed that backup to arrive now.

"I have them gathered in the conference room." Aikman glanced at him. "We'll join them and start the downloading of information, so to speak."

"I'll meet you there in fifteen. I need to wash the blood off my face and change clothes. We don't want them to see any sign of weakness. We need to present strength and unity so they'll understand the shift in power."

"Smart move. Fifteen minutes." Aikman suddenly stopped and turned back. "Ollie!"

One of his followers hustled up to join them. "Escort our friend Mr. Flynn to his personal lodging. Ensure he's in the conference room in fifteen minutes."

"Yes, sir." The man named Ollie turned his shaggy head to glare at Smith. "Let's go, Flynn."

Aikman didn't trust him as much as he'd let on. That made them even because Smith didn't trust him at all.

Outside was quiet. "Where is everyone?"

"They're in the detection center."

Smith was surprised the other man, Ollie, gave him an answer but he was glad he had. As much as Smith despised Prentiss, he did not want this day to turn into a mass killing of people whose only mistake was believing in the wrong man.

Walking across the quad was eerie. No sound. No movement. Nothing. The faces in the guard towers were unfamiliar to Smith. Aikman's people, no doubt. When they reached his cabin, Ollie went in, looked around and then waited outside, leaving the door open.

"If you go in the bathroom," he said to Smith, "don't close the door."

"Got it."

Smith grabbed fresh clothes and went into the tiny bathroom. He pulled the cell phone from his pocket, placed it on the sink, then did the same with the gun. When he'd dragged on the clean clothes, he looked to see that Ollie was still outside the door. He held the phone where it couldn't be seen from the door and sent a text message to 911. He had no idea if the 911 service in the area was able to receive text messages but, at the moment, it was his only available option. He couldn't risk making a call with Aikman's man right outside.

Once he'd sent the text, he deleted it. He set the phone to silent just in case the dispatcher tried to call him back, then slid it into his hip pocket. He shoved the weapon into his waistband at the small of his back, then washed his face.

His eyes and jaw were swollen, and he was reasonably sure he had a couple of cracked ribs, but things could be far worse.

He joined Ollie outside. "I'm ready."

The walk across the quad was the same as before, too quiet. Too still. They reached the headquarters and entered. Two guards were posted outside the door to the conference room. Ollie walked right up and opened the door and entered. Smith followed him.

The scene in the room brought him up short. The members of the Council lay on the floor in a neat line. All were dead, all had been shot once in the head.

His gaze swung to Aikman, who stood in the center of the room. Behind him someone was seated in a chair but Smith couldn't see who it was since Aikman blocked his view.

"I thought we were going to interrogate them." He glared at Aikman, his fingers itching to reach for the weapon in his waistband.

As if Ollie had sensed his thought, he plucked the weapon from Smith.

"That was far too much trouble," Aikman said. "It

seemed far easier to simply go to the head and learn everything straight from the source."

He stepped aside, revealing the person in the chair.

Rayford Prentiss.

"You weren't expecting to see me, were you, *Agent* Flynn?" Prentiss laughed. "Looks like this game of double-cross is going to turn out just fine for me." He glanced up at Aikman. "New blood is always a good thing."

SADIE DROPPED TO her haunches next to Sheriff Tanner. "Aikman and his people have taken over," she said, worry gnawing at her. "We can't wait, we have to move fast. The killing won't stop until we stop it."

The text message relayed to Tanner from the 911 dispatcher mentioned heavily armed men and numerous prisoners. Dozens were dead already.

Sadie's chest squeezed. The text had to be from Flynn, which meant, for now, he was still alive. She hoped he stayed that way until they could get in there and stop the killing.

The good news was, inside those walls were the leaders of the Resurrection and those of the *others*. This operation was going to stop two of the worst kind of extremist organizations in one fell swoop.

As much as she wanted to be grateful for that possibility, she couldn't help worrying about Flynn. She didn't want him to end up a casualty. She wanted to spend time with him. Time that didn't involve a mission or a race to stay alive.

Tanner nodded. "We're almost ready."

Sadie had been able to warn them about the scouts around the compound. Strangely they hadn't spotted any outside the walls. Had to have something to do with the takeover. Several bodies had been discovered.

Tanner put a hand on her arm. "We're moving." His gaze locked with hers. "But you're staying right here until we have the situation under control."

She drew her arm away from his touch. "No way, Sheriff. I'm going in with you."

He nodded to someone behind her and she shot to her feet only to come face-to-face with two female deputies.

"Ma'am," the dark-haired one said, "we'll go in as soon as we receive the all-clear signal from the sheriff."

Anger swirled through Sadie as she watched Tanner sprint forward. He'd double-crossed her. Dwelling on the reality would only distract her so she shrugged it off and focused on the events unfolding only yards away.

The two deputies moved in close next to her. One wore earbuds to listen in to the ongoing operation. The other watched through binoculars. Tanner hadn't left these two women with her because he didn't think women were as strong as men. Sadie had noticed seven female deputies. The other five had obviously gone in with Tanner. One of the women, she noticed, was very pregnant. She would have needed to stay away from live fire anyway.

Obviously she was fearless or she wouldn't be in these woods right now.

The echo of gunfire jerked her attention forward. The exchange was happening outside the entrance to the compound that had been built into the mountainside. Aikman no doubt had the entrance heavily guarded.

The sudden silence was more unnerving than the bursts of gunfire had been.

One minute turned into two and Sadie couldn't take it a second longer.

"Sorry, ladies, but I can't do this."

Sadie took off in a sprint. The deputy who wasn't pregnant rushed after her. Sadie ran harder. She disappeared into the thick trees and underbrush that camouflaged the entrance. The entrance stood open, dead followers lying on the ground.

Inside, Tanner's deputies had fanned out and were entering buildings.

Sadie palmed her weapon and headed for the headquarters building. As she neared the entrance, Tanner and the female caught up with her.

He pulled her next to a vehicle that had been parked there.

"What the hell are you trying to do, Buchanan?"

"They'll be in there." She jerked her head toward the building that was the headquarters. "This is where all the decisions are made. Where the Council meets."

"And you're certain Flynn will be in there."

His words hit like a blow to her midsection. She wasn't certain. She was guessing. Speculating. Concluding the most likely scenario.

"It makes the most sense." Sadie suddenly felt completely unsure.

Tanner used his radio to divert resources to their position. Sadie's heart thundered in her chest. What if she was wrong?

A single shot exploded beyond the walls of the headquarters building. Sadie might not have heard it if one of those moments of absolute silence hadn't settled around them beforehand. And the entry door stood open.

Tanner was the first to move. He burst through the open entrance.

Sadie was right behind him. The other deputy behind her.

With Tanner's glance at her, Sadie moved ahead of him and led the way to the conference room where she had been questioned by the Resurrection Council.

At the door Tanner gave her the signal to wait.

His next signal had Sadie and the deputy dropping into a crouch. Tanner banged on the closed door.

The door opened and a guard walked out.

Tanner rammed the muzzle of his weapon into his temple and pulled him aside.

Another guard rushed out. Sadie handled him.

"Well, well, it appears we have the proverbial standoff."

Sadie recognized the voice. Aikman.

"Do come in," he said. "Agent Flynn and I were just discussing our next move."

Leaving the two guards under the careful watch of the female deputy, Tanner and Sadie entered the conference room.

"Drop the weapon," Tanner ordered.

Sadie moved to one side of Tanner, who had a bead on his target. When her brain absorbed the image before her, her heart sank to the floor.

Aikman had Flynn on his knees. His weapon was pressed against Flynn's forehead. Nearby Prentiss sat in a chair, the bullet hole between his eyes leaking blood.

On the floor to her left was a line of dead bodies. The Council members.

"I'll drop the weapon when I'm safely on my way out of here," Aikman argued. "I'll turn Agent Flynn loose at that time, as well. Otherwise, I'm going to do the same thing to him that I did to Prentiss and the members of his esteemed Council."

As Tanner negotiated with the man who wasn't going to change his mind, Sadie made a decision. She lowered her weapon. "Take me instead. The Bureau is far more flexible in these negotiations than the ATF. Did we mention that both are here?"

Something flashed ever so briefly across Aikman's face. Flynn's was far easier to read: he was not happy with her offer.

"Back off," Tanner muttered to her.

Aikman grinned, obviously enjoying the dissention. "Well, aren't you the brave one? Come on over here and I'll let your friend go."

Sadie stepped forward.

"Don't do it, Buchanan," Tanner warned, his attention zeroed in on Aikman.

"It won't be my first bait and switch, Sheriff." She looked directly at Smith as she said this but quickly shifted her gaze to Aikman. "I'm not afraid of this guy."

Aikman smirked. "That's an astounding statement considering the dead bodies lining the room."

It was in that moment—that fraction of a second when Aikman thought he had to prove how scary he was—that Flynn made his move.

He twisted and dove into Aikman's knees.

Sadie dropped to the floor.

As if he'd been in on the plan from the beginning, Tanner fired one shot straight into Aikman's right shoulder. The fool's weapon fell from his suddenly limp fingers as he was propelled backward by Flynn.

Flynn grabbed Aikman's weapon and pushed to his feet. Aikman clutched at his shoulder, right where that major nerve center would be, and howled.

"Good shot," Flynn said to Tanner.

Sadie pushed to her feet but her knees had gone so weak she had no idea how she would remain upright.

Tanner took over the prisoner and Flynn walked toward her.

Her breath caught at the injuries to his face or maybe just at the sight of him moving toward her.

He was alive.

She was alive.

And they were getting out of here.

Flynn wrapped his arms around her and hugged her. The weapon in her right hand slipped to the floor. Her arms went around him.

"Thanks for coming back to rescue me," he murmured against her hair.

She turned her face up to him. "It's what I do."

He smiled then grimaced.

"Your face looks like hell," she pointed out.

"Feels like it, too."

THE NEXT SEVERAL hours were filled with rounding up prisoners and getting medical attention to those injured, as well as identifying the dead.

Flynn refused to bother with being checked out until the work was done. By the time they were off that mountain, Sadie was ready to drop.

George was in the DA's office making a deal. Sadie was glad. He'd paid in that tunnel for whatever he'd done wrong. Aikman was trying to work out a deal, as well. As it turned out the remains in that rock hole at Aikman's compound were those of Jack Kemp. The FBI had waited a long time to learn this information but both Ross and Tanner assured Sadie that Aikman wouldn't be getting any sort of deal beyond the possible setting aside of the death penalty.

Aikman was like Prentiss; he didn't deserve a deal. He deserved a long life behind bars where he'd have plenty of time to reflect on his bad judgment.

Deacon Ross had accompanied Levi Winters for his statement.

The place was crawling with federal agents.

Sadie's SAIC had called and made sure she was okay. Flynn had been sequestered to one of the interview rooms for his debrief. She had called her parents just to hear their voices. There was really no reason at this point for her to stay. She had done what she came here to do. She could go home. Maybe even call her sister.

Maybe if she told herself a couple more times there was no reason to stay she would talk herself into walking away without waiting for a chance to say goodbye to Flynn. He'd already thanked her for rescuing him. Goodbye wasn't actually necessary.

Except it felt necessary.

"Agent Buchanan."

Sadie looked up at the sound of her name. Cece Winters smiled as she walked through the door of the sheriff's office where Sadie had taken refuge. It was about the only room in the building that wasn't filled with agents and deputies. Tanner had told Sadie to make herself at home.

"Hey." Sadie returned the smile. "I'm sure they'll allow Levi to go home soon. This part takes a while sometimes."

Cece nodded as she sat down in the chair next to Sadie. "I wanted to thank you again for saving my brother not once but twice."

"He did his part," Sadie told her. "He's a good guy. A little confused maybe, but a good guy."

"Deacon and I plan on seeing that he gets back on the right track."

Sounded like the two were definitely a couple. Sadie had gotten that impression.

"Ladies."

Sadie's attention swung to the door once more. Flynn stood there, still looking a little worse for the wear.

Cece got to her feet. "I should see how Levi's doing."

She slipped out of the office and Flynn walked in. He closed the door behind him. Sadie looked from the closed door to him, her pulse starting to pound.

"I was afraid you'd left already."

"I was just getting ready to go." She tried to think what to say next. "It'll be good to get home."

He nodded. "I don't want to keep you." He exhaled a big breath. "But I was hoping we could get a bite to eat first. I don't know about you, but I'm starved."

As if her belly had just realized how empty it was, she nodded. "I could eat. Sure."

"Good."

They stood there for a moment without saying more. Sadie suspected he felt as awkward as she did. Neither of them was the kind of person who did this well.

"We both live in the Nashville area."

"Home sweet home." She felt heat rush to her cheeks. What a totally dumb thing to say.

He smiled, grimaced. "Yeah. Anyway, I hoped we might spend some time together. You know, get to know each other better."

She felt certain the grin that spread across her face said way too much about how happy his words made her. "I would like that very much."

"It's been a long time," he admitted, "since I've met anyone who understood this life…who made me want to get to know them better."

She was certain it would be entirely dorky for her to say the same thing. Instead, she put her hand in his. "I'm ready."

"I could take you home," he offered. "I heard you lost your car."

She laughed. "I would love for you to take me home."

That was all she needed to say. The rest would take care of itself.

* * * * *

Don't miss The Lies We Tell, *coming next month
from Debra Webb and MIRA Books!
Read on for an excerpt!*

The Lies We Tell
Debra Webb

RIP
Carlos Sanchez
September 3, 1948–October 24, 2019

Mr. Carlos Sanchez will be prepared for burial by DuPont Funeral Home. Friends and family may contact the funeral home for information regarding arrangements.

Chapter One

Franklin County Jail, Winchester, Tennessee
Thursday, October 25, 11:55 a.m.

Herman Carter looked old. So very old.

The past five months in jail awaiting trial had taken a toll on the seventy-one-year-old man. He'd lost weight, and his gray hair lacked its usual sheen. But it was his eyes that told the real story. Dull, listless, resigned.

Rowan DuPont felt no sympathy.

Renewed indignation tightened her lips. This man—a man she had known and trusted her entire life—had deceived her. He had taken advantage of her father…and betrayed so many people. For no other reason than greed. He could toss out his excuses about his wife's illness, but the truth was he had hurt people, using Rowan's family and the funeral home that had belonged to her family for a hundred and fifty years.

He deserved a far heavier punishment than she

imagined the court system would eventually dole out. *Eventually* being the key word. The trial wasn't scheduled to begin for another three months. The wheels of justice indeed moved slowly.

"Did you get my letters?" His voice sounded rusty, as if he rarely found a reason to use it.

"One every week," Rowan said, her voice stiff no matter that she had repeatedly attempted to relax. No matter that she did not want to be here this meeting was necessary. Furthermore, it was essential that she proceed with caution where her personal feelings were concerned. She needed him cooperative. Revealing her utter disdain would not aid toward that end.

Herman had written to her every week since his arrest. Until yesterday, she had not opened a single one of his letters. She had felt no desire to read anything he had to say. He could not be trusted in any capacity. Yet, unfortunately, he was the one person still living who was well versed in her family's history. He and her father had been best friends their whole lives. With her father dead going on a year now, Herman was the only person who might be able to help her.

For five months she had attempted to dissect her mother's journals. She had searched the funeral home as well as the living quarters from top to bottom. One by one she had questioned neighbors, business associates and anyone else who had known her parents. She had learned nothing useful toward her goal of uncovering the facts surrounding her sister's and her mother's deaths.

Perhaps the truth had died with her father.

Rowan still struggled with the loss of her father. The idea that he may have lied to her made adjusting to this new reality all the more difficult. A part of her refused to believe he had lied, no matter the rumors and innuendos she had encountered. The trouble was, she had to know for certain. Herman Carter, the man who had stolen body parts from the dead to broker on the black market, was the sole person on this planet who might be able to help her find the answers she sought. However hard she had searched to find the facts some other way, ultimately, she had realized *this* was her only choice. He was her final hope.

The thought of living with the uncertainty was something she was not prepared to do. Too much hinged on knowing the whole truth.

"Is that why you're here after all this time?" Herman asked, a spark of hope lighting his dark eyes. "Did my words persuade you to forgive me?"

Rowan clenched her jaw long enough to restrain the urge to laugh in the man's face. *Forgive him?* Not in this lifetime. All those weeks and months she had ignored his attempts at communicating. She had fully expected to continue on that course. Then, day before yesterday she had hit the wall, run out of viable options for finding answers. With no other alternative and however reluctantly, she began to open the letters and read each one, twice. They told her nothing useful. Rather, his words had repeatedly expressed how deeply sorry he was and how desperately he wanted her forgiveness.

Forgiveness was the one thing she could not give him. Beneath the table that separated them, her right knee started to bounce. She braced against the outward display of her emotions and said what needed to be said. "No."

The optimistic gleam that had appeared in his eyes died an abrupt death. "Then why are you here?"

"I'm here for information." Rowan squared her shoulders and stared straight into his defeated gaze. "You owe me the truth, Herman. The whole truth."

He shook his head, turned up his shackled hands. "I've told you and the police everything I did. I don't know what else I can do."

If only the issue were so simple. "I don't need the truth about what you did, Herman. We know what you did."

His shoulders drooped. "I don't understand what you're saying, Ro. I did bad things—but never at DuPont. Never. It was Woody who crossed that line, not me. I wouldn't have done that to Edward. And it only happened once. Even if Woody hadn't ended up dead, I guarantee you he wouldn't have done that again."

Really? She was supposed to be grateful he did his stealing from the dead at another funeral home? Unbelievable.

Focus, Ro.

Sticking with her agenda was imperative. The chief

of police had allowed her this extended visit with Herman for that specific purpose. She wasn't allowed to discuss the ongoing criminal case with Herman—not that she had any desire to do so. The chief—her longtime friend William "Billy" Brannigan—had allowed her to use this interview room rather than the usual visitation area with the metal bars and Plexiglas. Today could very well be her one chance to speak with Herman in this sort of setting. The elderly man was likely going away for the rest of his life.

Aim for the emotions. "My father considered you family, Herman. You meant a great deal to him." She moistened her lips. "To both of us."

"Edward meant a great deal to me. You mean the world to me, Ro."

His words were true. Rowan heard the sincerity in his tone, saw it in his face.

"I've found quite a few disturbing notes in my mother's journals. I'm convinced my parents were keeping a number of troubling secrets. I want to know what those secrets were."

"We all have secrets, Ro. Even you." He gave her a knowing nod. "It's part of being human."

Anger whipped through her before she could stop it. "None of my secrets involve murder. I'm certain you can understand how uncovering those sorts of secrets is of particular importance under the circumstances."

Circumstances. More frustration and anger swirled inside her. The circumstances involved a serial killer. One of the most prolific serial killers in recorded history. One who less than a year ago had been her dear friend. *Dr. Julian Addington*. The monster who murdered her father and dozens upon dozens of others.

A monster who, until recently, she had believed that she had brought into her father's life. Now she wasn't so sure.

She wasn't sure of anything, frankly.

"You've asked me repeatedly to forgive you," she reminded him. "If you want my forgiveness, then you need to help me." She had no intention of giving it even then, but she wasn't above dangling that particular carrot.

"I swear I'll help you any way I can," he promised. His earnest words urged her to trust him, to believe in him as she once had.

There was a time when she had considered Herman like a second father, a trusted and loving uncle. How could she not have recognized he was not the man she believed him to be? How had she missed the signs?

The same way you did with Julian.

A lump swelled in her throat. How was she supposed to get past the idea that she had been so damned blind? Her education and work experience were in the field of psychiatry. For years it had been her job to read people—to see what the homicide detectives on her team did not. She had been quite good at her job. Not once had she failed to solve the case…*until Julian*.

Julian and then Herman had proven her a fraud.

Herman owed her for that betrayal and by God she intended to collect.

"All right. I'll put together a timeline of dates and events. Billy will pass along my questions and then we'll meet again to discuss anything you recall about those dates and events. If you let me down—"

"I won't." Herman leaned forward. "Tell Billy to give you the key to my house," he urged. "Estelle was a stickler for keeping up the family photos. She documented every family event and special moment we shared with your family like a regular historian. You might find something useful there. Doesn't hurt to look."

To Rowan's knowledge there had been no evidence found in the Carter home and the house had subsequently been released by the department. Hopefully Billy wouldn't have a problem allowing her inside. Speaking of which—she glanced at the clock on the wall—Billy would be waiting for her by now. He'd promised her half an hour.

"I just need one favor from you."

Rowan drew back at his words, putting some distance between them. How dare he ask her for anything after all that he had done?

He held up his hands, the shackles rattling with the move. "It's not for me exactly. I'd like you to see that flowers are put on Estelle's grave every year on her birthday. It's coming up next month and I've worried that I won't be able to arrange the delivery. Your father always did that for your mother and I surely would like to do it for my sweet Estelle."

She wanted to say no but that would be wrong. It wasn't Estelle's fault her husband had hurt others. His actions were part of the reason Estelle was dead and he was living with that painful fact. No, that wasn't entirely true. The cancer had been killing her; she simply ended things early after learning what her husband had done. It was bad enough to face the pain of the disease each day. What woman would want to deal with an investigation into the criminal affairs of the man she had loved and trusted? Giving up the battle had been easier.

"Fine. I'll ensure that Estelle has flowers every year on her birthday." Rowan would have done it anyway.

Herman nodded. "Thank you. That's all I ask."

Rowan slid her chair back from the table and stood. A few feet away, outside the door, two guards waited to return the old man watching her to his cell. She was beyond ready for that to happen. She needed out of this room. Away from another of the men in her life who had betrayed her. Except she needed his help. Her personal feelings had to take a back seat for now.

She pushed in the chair she'd vacated. "I'll be in touch again soon."

When she turned her back to him he spoke again.

"Your daddy was a good man, Ro. Whatever else you believe, believe that."

Rowan forced one foot in front of the other until she reached the door. She walked out of the room. The guards went inside to reclaim custody of their prisoner. Rowan kept moving down the corridor without looking back. She didn't stop until she found Billy.

"How'd it go?" he asked.

She shrugged. "Well enough, I suppose."

Billy pushed away from the wall where he'd been waiting. "You can tell me all about it over lunch."

Rowan had no appetite, but she'd learned over the past several months not to mention details such as those to Billy. He worried about her, fussed over her. As much as she appreciated their friendship, that aspect was often frustrating. Outside work, she had lived a solitary life in Nashville. Her evenings had most always been spent hovered over a case file until she fell asleep. The occasional night out with friends was always with *work* friends and even those occasions were rare.

"Lunch sounds good."

He glanced at her. "You're getting better at hiding how you really feel."

So he was on to her. "Lunch has never been high on my priority list."

It was true. She often forgot to stop for lunch. Even as a child, she and her twin sister would play and never think to stop and eat. Their mother had fussed when they finally made their way home. Not that Norah DuPont was much of a cook. Generally, Rowan and Raven had prepared their own meals. But that detail didn't prevent Norah from saying a mouthful if she happened to be home and noticed the time of day when her daughters finally showed up. Norah had been a little scattered and she'd spent a lot of time traveling. Their father had always been the primary parent. Which was likely why both she and Raven had been well versed in the preparation of a body for burial before they were old enough to date.

Billy opened the passenger-side door of his truck. "Burt called. He's sending business your way."

Burt Johnston was the county coroner. He also operated two veterinary clinics in Franklin County. Since the exposure of the black market body part brokering a good number of folks in the community who passed away were transported to a Tullahoma funeral home for their services. Gardner's, the only other funeral home in Winchester, had almost gone out of business under the weight of the lawsuits. No matter that they had avoided any lawsuits, DuPont's hadn't slipped by unscathed. Clientele had dropped off considerably.

Fortunately for Rowan, her overhead costs were minimal, allowing her to ride out the storm. Gardner apparently wasn't so lucky.

"Anyone we know?" she asked.

Winchester was a small town. Most everyone knew everyone else. The small-town atmosphere was part of the reason Rowan had been determined to move on to a larger city when she left for college. But she'd learned the hard way that she couldn't hide who she was simply by expanding the number of faces surrounding her. Strangely, she had decided she liked the idea of knowing the folks around her. Less likely to be so blatantly betrayed.

Then again, there was Herman. Knowing him inordinately well hadn't prevented her blindness to his betrayal.

No, Rowan decided. What she liked about being back in Winchester was that she had grown up here. She had been labeled and pigeonholed at a very young age as the undertaker's daughter. Though she was the undertaker now, folks still saw her as the undertaker's daughter and she understood exactly what was expected of her and where she stood in the community. Whatever she did or didn't do, little would change in terms of how folks viewed her. Strangely, there was something comforting about the status quo.

"Never heard of him," Billy said in answer to her question about the new intake. "One Carlos Sanchez, seventy-one. A neighbor discovered him, deceased, in his apartment over in Bell View."

Bell View? Rowan didn't know Carlos Sanchez but she did know Bell View. Run-down, roach-infested apartments and derelict houses, operated by the closest thing to a slumlord that resided in Winchester.

"Cause of death?" Couldn't be murder or the coroner wouldn't be releasing the body so quickly. He would instead be sending the man to Nashville for an autopsy.

"Heart attack."

"Any family?"

"Nope. His friend showed Burt and my officer a letter of instruction Sanchez had told him about. The letter expressly instructed that his body was to be taken care of by DuPont Funeral Home and stated that the insurance policy to cover the costs had been taken out with an insurance company downtown. The policy number is in the letter."

"I guess the man knew what he wanted."

Lots of people made advance arrangements. They just didn't generally live in Bell View.

Rowan had learned from experience that the one thing you could count on was that life never failed to toss out the occasional surprise.

She wondered what other surprises she would discover about Mr. Carlos Sanchez.

Get 4 FREE REWARDS!

We'll send you 2 FREE Books plus 2 FREE Mystery Gifts.

Harlequin Intrigue® books feature heroes and heroines that confront and survive danger while finding themselves irresistibly drawn to one another.

FREE
Value Over
$20

INTRIGUE

*Waking in the middle of a war zone, Jane Doe
has no memory of who she is or who she can trust.
When she meets former elite Force Recon member
Gus Walsh, she finds that trusting him is her only
chance at finding answers.*

Read on for a sneak preview of
Driving Force,
the fourth installment of the thrilling
Declan's Defenders *series by* New York Times
and USA TODAY *bestselling author Elle James.*

CHAPTER ONE

She struggled to surface from the black hole trying to suck
her back down. Her head hurt and she could barely open her
eyes. Every part of her body ached so badly she began to
think death would be a relief. But her heart, buried behind
bruised and broken ribs, beat strong, pushing blood through
her veins. And with the blood, the desire to live.

Willing her eyes to open, she blinked and gazed through
narrow slits at the dirty mud-and-stick wall in front of her.
Why couldn't she open her eyes more? She raised her hand
to her face and felt the puffy, blood-crusted skin around
her eyes and mouth. When she tried to move her lips, they
cracked and warm liquid oozed out on her chin.

Her fingernails were split, some ripped down to the quick,
and the backs of her knuckles looked like pounded hamburger

meat. Bruises, scratches and cuts covered her arms.

She felt along her torso, wincing when she touched a bruised rib. As she shifted her search lower, her hands shook and she held her breath, feeling for bruises, wondering if she'd been assaulted in other ways. When she felt no tenderness between her legs, she let go of the breath she'd held in a rush of relief.

She pushed into a sitting position and winced at the pain knifing through her head. Running her hand over her scalp, she felt a couple of goose egg–sized lumps. One behind her left ear, the other at the base of her skull.

A glance around the small cell-like room gave her little information about where she was. The floor was hard-packed dirt and smelled of urine and feces. She wore a torn shirt and the dark pants women wore beneath their burkas.

Voices outside the rough wooden door made her tense and her body cringe.

She wasn't sure why she was there, but those voices inspired an automatic response of drawing deep within, preparing for additional beatings and torture.

What she had done to deserve it, she couldn't remember. Everything about her life was a gaping, useless void.

The door jerked open. A man wearing the camouflage uniform of a Syrian fighter and a black hood covering his head and face stood in the doorway with a Russian AK-47 slung over his shoulder and a steel pipe in his hand.

Don't miss
Driving Force *by Elle James,*
available October 2019 wherever
Harlequin® books and ebooks are sold.

www.Harlequin.com

HIEXP0919

Need an adrenaline rush from nail-biting tales
(and irresistible males)?

Check out **Harlequin Intrigue®**,
Harlequin® Romantic Suspense and
Love Inspired® Suspense books!

New books available every month!

CONNECT WITH US AT:

Facebook.com/groups/HarlequinConnection

Facebook.com/HarlequinBooks

Twitter.com/HarlequinBooks

Instagram.com/HarlequinBooks

Pinterest.com/HarlequinBooks

ReaderService.com

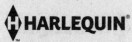

**ROMANCE WHEN
YOU NEED IT**

SGENRE2018R

Love Harlequin romance?

DISCOVER.

Be the first to find out about promotions,
news and exclusive content!

Facebook.com/HarlequinBooks

Twitter.com/HarlequinBooks

Instagram.com/HarlequinBooks

Pinterest.com/HarlequinBooks

ReaderService.com

EXPLORE.

Sign`up for the Harlequin e-newsletter and
download a free book from any series at
TryHarlequin.com.

CONNECT.

Join our Harlequin community to share
your thoughts and connect with other
romance readers!
Facebook.com/groups/HarlequinConnection

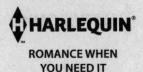

ROMANCE WHEN
YOU NEED IT

HSOCIAL2018